THE BRIDE WORE RED

tales
of a
cross-cultural
family

Robbie Clipper Sethi

Picador USA
New York

Picador® is a U.S. registered trademark and is used by St. Martin's Press under license from Pan Books Limited.

Library of Congress Cataloging-in-Publication Data

Sethi, Robbie Clipper.
     The bride wore red / Robbie Clipper Sethi.
          p.   cm.
     ISBN 0-312-16795-4
     I. Title.
PS3569.E767B75   1997
813'.54—dc21   97-15516
                                                                 CIP

First published in the United States by Bridge Works Publishing Company

First Picador USA Edition: November 1997

10   9   8   7   6   5   4   3   2   1

The following stories have appeared elsewhere in a different form: "The Bride Wore Red" in *Mademoiselle* and *Grazia* (in Italian translation); "The Pilgrimage" in *The Massachusetts Review*; "The White-Haired Girl" in *California Quarterly*; "Gudrun's Saga" as "Coping with Islam" in *In the Mail*; "Grace" in *The Atlantic Monthly*, *The Voice* (Iowa Indo-American Association), *New Worlds of Literature*, second ed. (Norton, 1994), *Breaking Up Is Hard to Do* (Crossing Press, 1994), and *Stree* (Woman) (in Marathi translation); "Bridgewater Burning Ground" in *Ascent*; "The Housewarming" in *Alaska Quarterly Review* and *Experiencing Race, Class and Gender in the United States* (Mayfield, 1992); and "A White Woman's Burden" in *The New Review*.

➤ Acknowledgments ◄

I would like to thank the New Jersey State Council on the Arts for two fellowships in prose, the National Endowment for the Arts, and Rider University, whose support contributed to the writing of *The Bride Wore Red*. Thanks to my colleagues and students at Rider who read parts of this manuscript and encouraged me, to Kimberly Witherspoon, and to the editors of various periodicals who considered and commented on my work. Thanks also to Kathleen Kisner, Lester Goldberg, Debbie Lee Wesselmann, Susan Land, and Barbara Phillips, whose close reading contributed to the development of this book as well as to my development as a writer. Thanks most of all to my husband and son, who have given me the time to write.

➤ Contents ◀

THE ❧ Extended Singh Family ❧

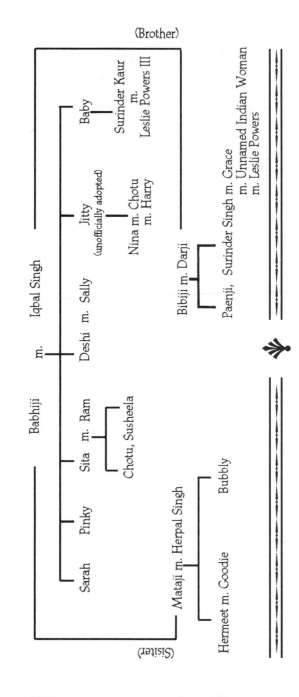

THE BRIDE
WORE
RED

The Bride Wore Red

You've stayed with Deshi because he is the only man you ever wanted who did not require a wife to play dumb to make him feel smarter. Though you are rather small, he is not much bigger, so in this relationship the big man's impulse to protect the little girl has been minimal. More: you've always thought yourself exotic, the one who didn't belong. When you told the boy next door that you were marrying an Indian, he laughed and said, *Sally, I always knew you'd end up with a foreigner; you never could stand the typical American boy.* Now you're with the man you've always wanted. In a place you don't belong.

As you step off the plane, in front of Deshi but close enough so that they'll know you are together, you are confronted by a sea of swarthy faces peering through the chain links of the runway fence. Saris flash color in the yellowish airport lights; turbans bulge on the heads of several bearded men. You cannot guess which ones belong to Deshi. You turn to him for

1

reassurance. He's lost, forcing half a smile, the rest of his face appearing as bewildered as you feel. When you turn around again a woman behind the fence is hanging limp in the arms of two bearded, turbaned men. "Oh, my God, she's sick," says Deshi, and that's the last you understand as he rushes you into customs. He speaks to an official in a language you don't understand. You regret that you have not learned the language of his childhood.

People are jostling and shoving for their luggage. You have never seen bigger suitcases in your life. Skinny boys wheel them in from the tarmac. Thickset men, thin men with paunches straining against their silk shirts, round-hipped, greasy-haired women drag the bags across the dusty, concrete floor. The airport smells like a cross between the subway on a summer afternoon and the spices Deshi uses when he cooks for you.

You've been awake for forty-seven hours. Your eyes burn. Your arms and legs ache, craving both movement and inertia at once. It's three o'clock in the morning, Delhi time.

You and Deshi separate to go through customs. An official silently checks your papers. Beyond customs stand the same two men who had held up the falling woman at the fence. Their stomachs stick out comically, as if they had been successfully implanted with embryos. The woman, not so thin herself, is still struggling with them, crying. Deshi doesn't have to tell you; she's his mother. He says something to the customs agent in his line; the official looks over his shoulder and turns back to Deshi's passport with a nod. Deshi runs to his mother, stoops in front of her, and puts his fingers on her feet. Passed into customs, you take a few steps toward them. The older man — Deshi's father — makes a show to lift Deshi off the floor. When Deshi stands, the woman pulls him toward her chest and sobs. Over his shoulder, with her eyes tightly closed, she makes kissing noises, but her lips make contact only with the hot, dusty air. The men wait. You are not sure who the younger man is. His beard is not as gray, and the flesh on his face is not pulled so tightly by his beard, which is slicked down with what looks like mustache wax and hair spray and tied beneath his double chin. Deshi introduces you without telling you who either of them is. The younger one stretches his arm around your shoulder and you smell his sweat. The old man tries to catch his wife again as she falls to the floor.

Deshi bends over her, speaking softly in Punjabi. The old man pinches her nose; the young man only touches her ankles and she straightens out her legs. A customs official joins you and shouts something in Hindi. He pushes you closer to the prone woman. She opens her eyes, looks directly into your face, and closes her eyes again.

Though you have finished medical school, Deshi does not ask for your advice. You've seen people faint, you've seen them die. This woman isn't dying; she hasn't even fainted.

The men pick her up and walk her out of customs through the double doors, filthy with finger marks, into the waiting room. As the doors close behind them, you see that the lobby is even more crowded than customs. You see the faces of women, leaning over to look inside the door. You see children straining at their mothers' saris, screaming. You'd like to scream yourself at this hour, in this mess. "Does she have a preexisting medical condition?" you ask.

Deshi says, "She's just a little over-emotional."

Your own mother, to your knowledge, has never fainted. The only time you ever saw her cry was the day that Kennedy was shot. You came home from school and saw her watching a replay of the Dallas motorcade, a tissue to her eyes. You were baffled. She didn't know this man. He was a politician; he had run against another politician; a politician had run with him; there were millions of politicians ready to take his place.

You have been accused of coldness, but that was only by a roommate who took your love life more seriously than you did. That was before you met Deshi. He's his calm, collected self as he leads you to the luggage.

"I wish I'd brought my blood pressure sleeve," you say.

"It's just the shock," says Deshi.

You know what he means, but you don't say anything. For weeks you tried to convince him to write a letter to his family explaining that he and a woman he had known for several years were planning to be married and that she was coming with him on his first trip to New Delhi in ten years. He procrastinated until it was too late to write. Finally he telephoned, but only to tell them what time the plane was landing. At the time, you asked, "Why didn't you tell them you were bringing me?"

"They wouldn't understand."

Now *you* understand. You wonder where you'll spend the night, and with more than a little relief you realize it's too late for bed. By the time your luggage gets through customs, nothing illegal, nothing to declare, it is four A.M. You squeeze through the waiting crowd and feel around your shoulders the cool, wet arms of a plump woman. Your first impulse is to shake them off, but you force yourself to return a little squeeze. When you were a baby, your mother has told you, you refused to be cuddled. When she tried to hold you, you screamed. The woman abandons you just before you scream and smiles through the lipstick caked on her crackling lips. "I am the sister," she says.

I am the wife-to-be, you want to say, but you say, "Hi. I'm Sally."

Another woman grabs you, thinner than the last. You recognize the name of a third sister. Then sister after sister embraces you, all of them short and busty like Deshi's mother. By the time they're through, you feel like you've been gangbanged by a pack of virgins.

Deshi's mother looks at you and goes limp again, while a sister shouts at her in Punjabi. Another sister lunges for the body; so many sisters crowd around, it's a wonder she can breathe. Someone pinches her nose, straightens her legs, and she moans. "Mummy's little bit upset," a sister says smiling.

It's then that you see the small children clinging to the sisters' saris and baggy pants. "What are you doing?" one says. "Say hello to your auntie."

You want to tell her you're not married

yet, but you're afraid someone might faint if you so much as mention the M-word.

The children cry. One of them turns her face into the sister's leg. It occurs to you they would be cute if they were a little leaner. Some of them are wearing earrings; some you think are boys have long, braided hair.

You drag yourself out of the airport while Deshi, his father, and his brother-in-law guide the mother outside. Boys in khaki with rifles stand guard. One opens the door of a taxi, and for a moment you're afraid all of you might squeeze inside. Someone pushes you in. You sit between Deshi and one of his sisters, your thighs pressed between her soft flesh on the one side and his bony muscle on the other. One of the children, sitting on her mother's lap, kicks your knee repeatedly while she sucks her hand. You used to like children. But four years of college and three years of medical school have removed you thoroughly from them, and you are not looking forward to your pediatric rotation.

Deshi's mother is moaning in the front seat. Deshi is trying to smile. You smile back, feeling no joy. When his mother starts talking, he loses the smile. "Translate," you say.

He says no.

"She is worried that my brother is so thin," the sister says.

You have always suspected that as a child Deshi was force-fed. His fear of overeating borders on the pathological. But you like that. Every other man you've ever had expected to be fed twice as often as you even thought of food. It occurs to you too late to block the thought that Deshi's sister might be lying to cover up a more devastating comment. Either that, or she's trying to make you feel guilty for starving her brother. In spite of your better judgment, you feel guilty.

At five o'clock in the morning the airport road is thick with cars and buses. Men in army blankets walk along the weedy shoulders, long staffs in their hands. You are reminded of the plodding multitudes in the Bible. A little scared, you stare, dying to get out of the car and see India. As the taxi approaches the city, traffic increases, especially pedestrians. You drive around a circle. Billboards as big as drive-in movie screens advertise fabric, film stars, baby formula. Well-fed, made-up faces stare down at you, a third eye dotted on their foreheads. Deshi's sisters wear the same red dot above their eyes, smudgy from their sweat. On the morning of your wedding they will paint a dot on your forehead too, pink because you are so white. But before they consent to your marriage, Deshi's mother must faint a few more times. Every time she looks at you.

That afternoon you try to take a nap, but it's cut short by people talking, shouting, even singing just outside your door. When you stumble into an enclosed courtyard in the back of the house, you realize that the talking has been coming from just outside your room. They quiet down when you walk in; the mother faints.

Deshi, who's been up for two days and looks it, asks you if you'd like a drink. You accept eagerly, thinking that even grain alcohol wouldn't be strong enough to get you through this. You whisper, "I'm sorry I came."

"Are you kidding?" he says. "My sisters love you. They've been on the phone all morning. The wedding's set."

You're not sure their plans console you. Deshi pours some beer into a stainless steel cup, explaining, "My aunts are coming over. It wouldn't do to let them know you're drinking."

As you drain your cup and hold it out for more, it occurs to you that Deshi hasn't asked about wedding arrangements. "I don't think your mother wants you to marry me," you say, tempted to give in to a little hysteria of your own.

"She's insisting on it," Deshi says. "She

thinks we're already married, and she wants to get us to the temple as fast as possible, so that we'll be married in the eyes of God."

"Tell me about God again," you say. You've never had much of a god yourself. You think maybe her god might console you.

"The Sikh god," your lover says, "is truth."

The truth is, you spend every spare moment in the bathroom, the only place you can be alone, and every time you look at your remarkably white face in the mirror, you burst out crying. You don't have the solitude to figure out why. There's only one bathroom. You don't even have the time to wonder what would happen if you washed your face, combed your hair and walked confidently into the family circle with the painful announcement that you have decided not to get married after all because you don't want children, Deshi already has a green card, and you've been enjoying connubial bliss just fine without the approval of God, the family, or the IRS. But you've come this far. You've got to get it over with before you go back home, because you don't know when you're coming here again.

But before you can get it over with, you have to buy the sari. When Deshi's mother has recovered from her fainting spells, she sends one of her daughters into the bathroom to get you. "Come," she says, not telling you where you are going. You trail along, hoping you will see something of India. They walk you around the corner where an old black taxi waits to drive you through the crowded streets. The masses of pedestrians, the reds, blues, oranges, and yellows of their clothes, the cows, the three-wheeled motor scooters, rickety old trucks, and boxlike cars turn your neck to rubber by the time you reach the shop, where you sit on the floor while a well-fed Sikh throws yards of fabric over your knees, chattering in Punjabi and smiling as he hurls out another six yards. A young boy brings you tea, staring through not only your Western clothing but also your white skin. Finally Deshi's mother stops the steady stream of fabric. Her knobbed and gnarled hands smooth a piece of vermilion silk dotted with golden flowers. You don't know what she's saying, but it's the most upbeat tone she's used since you met her. You wish the mood would last, but she looks at you and says something glum that makes the shopkeeper and her daughters laugh.

You venture an inquiry.

A daughter translates, "She says you are so thin that only half a sari will cover you."

You're flattered. You have been fighting the superior American diet all your life to maintain a twenty-two-inch waist, and now you will be showing off your midriff just like Deshi's sister, whose tires of flesh pour out from under her sari blouse as if she didn't know that people were starving in India.

In and out of cabs, on the way to sari shops and jewelry stores, you see the starving. Wizened faces stare at you like children, begging hands approach your face. You spend most of your time in the house, exhausted by the shopping, wondering where Deshi is while people you don't know drop by to inspect you. In front of the house, three steps down from the veranda, beggars congregate, having heard that there will be a wedding. Your future relatives, afraid that envy might destroy your chances to have sons, throw pennies to the ragged.

On your wedding day Deshi's sisters part your hair in the middle. They insist you line your eyes with kohl, though the black smudges look like bruises under your blue eyes. They smear your lips with sticky red lipstick. It smells like the kind you used to steal from your mother's dresser, and it occurs to you that the last time you wore lipstick you were nine years old and dressed in your mother's white peignoir for a game of "here comes the bride." After they have squeezed your breasts into a blouse so tight that you can hardly move your arms, so short it does not cover all your ribs, you step into a long cotton petticoat, and one of the sisters ties its drawstring top so close that you fear for your circulation. Tucking one end into your waist, they wrap the six yards of vermilion silk around you so that you cannot walk without stepping on the spun-gold border. You cannot free your left arm. They bring out a bowl full of bangles soaked in milk and brush-burn your knuckles forcing them on. The room is filling up with chattering, laughing women. To the bangles on your wrists they tie gold ornaments, larger versions of the Hindustani earrings with which you used to load down your earlobes in high school. Now you are ready to be married.

You don't know where Deshi is until you get to the temple. Even there, you're not sure they haven't brought another little guy in his blue suit, because they've stuffed his head into a red turban and covered his face with a veil made out of marigold garlands and golden fringe. "So no one will give him the evil eye," a sister says, as she draws the end of your sari over your forehead. At least in India the groom gets to wear the veil, you think, grateful that this foreign ceremony has freed you from the hypocrisy of wearing white. You are relieved that your parents have opted out of the celebration.

The confusion would give your mother a heart attack. And you have always promised your father that, since he shelled out thousands for your education, when you were ready to get married you would elope, paying for the license from your own pocket.

A harmonium is playing. You try to walk down the aisle, but you have had to leave your shoes outside — platforms, because in 1975 in India they are the latest thing — and now you have four more inches of hemline than you counted on when they measured your sari from your waist to the floor. The end of your sari is pinned to your hair. Your head must stay covered, they tell you, out of respect for the book. You are not entirely unfamiliar with this concept of book worship, as your Protestant ancestors risked persecution just to read the Bible. But you have never bowed down and thrown paper money at a book.

You are standing next to the man you left America with five days ago. As his father takes off the veil that has protected Deshi's face from envy, you wonder who he is, the son of these book worshipers, or the man who paid for your vodka gimlets between dances and agreed that a little knowledge *is* a dangerous thing, that the direct pursuit of pleasure *is* ultimately self-defeating, and that extremism in the pursuit of democracy is still extreme. You stand awhile. You sit down. They get you up again. When they want you to move, they push. It's all so easy. You don't have to know the language. You walk around the book. At some point in the ceremony, Deshi's mother, who hasn't fainted once though it's hotter than hell in the temple, becomes your mother-in-law, and the congregation showers you with rose petals. Hallelujah. Out in the courtyard, where you can put your shoes on again, everybody eats, and your mother-in-law, who hasn't eaten in public since you arrived, makes a big show of feeding you seven spoonfuls of a dessert of carrots and evaporated milk. You suppress a gag. You wonder how you ever got into the courtyard of this stucco and gold temple, wrapped up in six yards of red and gold fabric that hides your feet but leaves your midriff bare. Your mother-in-law has wrapped a veil around her head, and every now and then she wipes her face with it and mutters to anyone who will listen. You understand only her eyes. She had to bear the births of all these daughters before she made a son, and with a man she'd never seen before they were married for life. She gazes at her son like a lover. He hasn't disappointed her a bit. *You* have. She looks at you through a veneer of resignation. Her eyes glow; her lower lip is barely trembling. And well she might fear you. Her son has defied her to risk this marriage between East and West. And isn't that what you wanted in a man all along?

⇒ The Pilgrimage ⇐

We were about to light a fire in the street, a surefire way to get arrested in New Jersey. In New Delhi it's a way to celebrate Lohri, the last day of winter, a Hindu holy day that my niece was telling me about: "There was this boy. He wanted to worship Vishnu. But his father wouldn't let him. I mean, the father thought his son should worship him. But the boy loved Vishnu. He was a real fan."

"How ridiculous," her father said. "You cannot say 'fan.' Do you think Vishnu was a film star?"

"It's the same thing," she whined.

"It is not the same. Susheela, no one worships film stars. You are confusing Sally Auntie. Just tell her why we are celebrating. She does not know. How can she? She is not a Hindu."

I was not a Sikh either, like my husband, whose sister had converted to marry Ram. I was not much of anything, though my ancestors had all been Protestant. Deshi and I had come to

17

India for our second visit, five years after our Indian wedding.

The household servant, a five-foot-two tough guy with narrow, Nepali eyes, slunk out of the house and offered a tray of popcorn to Ram's mother, who had wedged herself between the aluminum arms of a lawn chair on the sidewalk. Extracting her hand from her shawl, she took a handful; then with a scowl she waved the servant away. He hurried over to my mother-in-law, my father-in-law, then my sister-in-law, Sita. "Yummy!" my nephew said as he stuffed a handful in his mouth.

Sita pulled on his hand. "Are you stupid? We must bless that first."

The servant poured a cup of cooking oil on the firewood — five fruit crates stacked up taller than he by a foot — and threw a match. Flames shot up to the telephone and power lines festooned above the curb. Sita passed us the tray and told me, "Throw eight handfuls, then eat little bit." The crates collapsed, scattering sparks and burning brands across the dusty street.

Three men peddled by on a bicycle, shouting in Hindi. Deshi laughed. "What did they say?" I asked.

"Lohri was last night."

We'd suspected as much. We had heard the drums of wandering musicians, their singing at the neighbors' fires. The city air had filled up with twice as much smoke as usual, and we'd watched from the roof, caught up in Ram's argument about the proper night to celebrate.

"It is tonight," Ram insisted. "I asked four people in my office. Lohri is always on the thirteenth, January."

"It starts at midnight, Papa," Susheela said.

"Officially it may start after midnight," he said. "You do not know these simple people, Sally. They do not have the patience to celebrate on the proper day."

"The same thing happens every year," my nephew whined, pulling a piece of smoldering wood out of the fire. His mother shrieked, "Chotu!" and chased him for half a block, then staggered back on her high heels, gasping. Chotu came back giggling and ran around the smoking crates.

"We must leave at eight o'clock sharp," Ram said. "Five hours driving, one hour to eat. We will reach Hardwar by two. We can have our tea, then go directly to the temples. That means you must be up by seven. Deshi, do you think you will be ready?"

"No problem," my husband said.

"You cannot be used to getting up so early."

"Are you kidding? I commute to New York at six every morning."

"Six? So early? In America everyone works too hard. But you are on holiday. You must be sleeping late."

"We'll be up."

"You must. We must leave at eight o'clock sharp."

We harbored few hopes of Ram's arriving at all. He was constantly making plans, only to break them when his car refused to start. But in Deshi's parents' house, it was impossible to sleep in. At dawn the pigeons started in the courtyard just outside the bedroom door. My mother-in-law shouted for the servants. Hawkers began calling out the names of the vegetables and fruits they wheeled through the streets. By the time that Ram telephoned to say he'd be a little late, we were already dressed. We took a walk in the hope that he might come and we would miss him.

It was a holy day at the Sikh temple on the edge of the market. A loudspeaker was broadcasting a song in the thin voices of children, who must have been sitting underneath the big gold dome where Deshi and I had been married. Deshi and his sister had rebelled against their religion. In the United States Deshi had become fastidious about the haircuts that Sikhism prohibited; his sister had changed her Sikh name and given up monotheism for holy fire and little brass idols.

"Shall we go in?" Deshi asked.

I shrugged. "I don't have anything to cover my head."

On our way back we passed Chotu dribbling a soccer ball in the street. I didn't see Ram's car, so I assumed the plans were canceled. In the courtyard behind the house we found Susheela and Sita sitting with Deshi's mother in the sun, all three of them displaying brilliant, wide Punjabi trousers and candy-colored tunics in the style of Western shifts. "So?" Sita said, shading her eyes. "Gone for a round?"

"Where's Ram?" I asked. "Are we going?"

"We will go."

I sat next to her on a low-slung chair woven out of ropes. Susheela put down her movie magazine and smiled. I took out my book, a thriller I had bought on the sidewalk, and for another half hour I wandered through the streets of Istanbul.

At eleven Ram strolled through the house, a smile stretched across his face. "Come, Sally, we are going. Where is Deshi?"

We threw our coats and bag into the trunk of Ram's 1959 Padmini sedan, actually a

Fiat, assembled in India. Ram had bought it from his cousin's husband's brother, who just happened to be Deshi's best friend's father. Fourteen years ago Deshi might have cruised New Delhi in this very car.

Sita and Susheela squeezed into the front seat; Deshi, Chotu, and I sat in the back, in that order. I leaned against the window, filmed with a strip of blue plastic, protection against the summer sun that would not bake the glass and blind the eyes for two more months. Neighborhoods, all the same pale blue, rolled by. "Deshi," Ram said. "Do you recognize this colony? You went to college here."

"Sally Auntie, there is Qutab Minar," Susheela said, "where Hindu ladies come to pray for sons."

"They do not pray for sons," Ram said. "Qutab Minar is a Muslim monument."

"They do too pray for sons."

The going was slow. Every time we pulled up to a light, the engine died.

"I spent thousand rupees on this car," said Ram. "There cannot be anything wrong."

The engine strained to make it up to cruising speed, almost dying on the Yamuna River bridge. Even downhill horns blared in our wake.

"This is Ghaziabad," Ram said. "We

have left New Delhi. Shall we stop for a drink?"

"No," I said. In an hour we had gone seven miles.

We bypassed the bypass and drove past lean-tos full of scooters, cars, and trucks. Ram pulled into a hard-packed lot. Tin cans, bottles, crates, and a few battered cars littered the dried mud around a concrete shack. "I'll just get these chaps to have a look," Ram said.

He brought back a short, squat man, his shirt and pants at least three days black with grease. Ram started the motor while the man lifted the hood, a smile stretched across his full-moon face. They exchanged a few words, and Ram drove the car beneath a row of emaciated mimosas. Deshi got out of the car; Chotu followed.

"He will fix it in one hour," Ram said.

I took out my book. The mechanics took out the air filter, carburetor, half a dozen other parts. Sita sat in the front seat staring at the trees. Susheela whined: "Why do we have to break down in a place with no shops or hotels?"

Deshi stuck his head in the window. "It's a gasket."

"The head?" I said. "No one can fix a head in an hour."

Ram peered in the other side. "No one

23

can fix a head in an hour," he said. "Very funny, Sally. Deshi, this Sally is very funny."

"Have you ever seen two guys take an entire car apart by the roadside?" Deshi asked me.

"In America they do not fix," Ram said. "In America they throw away. Isn't it? Throw away society. That's what they —"

"Sally Auntie, Sally Auntie," Susheela cried.

"Look," Sita shouted. "Up there! On the roof!"

A pack of monkeys, like squirrels, crawled down the corrugated roof of the shack to see if the tools and rags littered around the car might be edible. They stared hungrily while Chotu dug stones out of the dust, then drifted away, Chotu just managing to miss the last one.

In two hours we were on the road again, through Ghaziabad and into the countryside, where cultivated yellow fields of mustard, back home the first weed of spring, gave way to rows and rows of spiky sugar cane, lined up like yuccas at a flea market. The air was thick with burning dung and boiling molasses. We slowed down to pass men on bicycles, women on foot with enormous bundles on their heads, and bullock carts loaded to the rim with cane. In the middle of the fields, a sign rose up: Tijuana Cafe.

"Would you like something to drink?" Ram asked.

"I do, I do," Susheela said, while Chotu rattled something off in Hindi. "I'm utterly parched."

"I think everybody needs a drink," said Ram.

Not me. After the way Ram had abused the starter on the way out, I was afraid to stop anywhere.

He cut the motor. I held my breath.

An open-air restaurant stood behind a few thorny sprigs of bushes that seemed never to have put out roses. Deshi took a path to the rest rooms in the back. Ram asked me what I wanted. Seven beverages were on the menu, printed in English and Hindi on a board above the counter. According to the counter boys, smiling over trays of sticky sweets and oily snacks, four out of seven were available. "I'm not thirsty," I said.

"This cannot be," said Ram. "Everyone is thirsty." He ordered a bottle of milk flavored with rosewater syrup. Sita sucked at a box full of mango juice. Susheela stared at the menu board and moaned. Chotu insisted on a Campa Cola, born the year the Indian government sent Coke the way of the British. "Sally, you must," Ram said.

I scanned the list for bottled water, the

only kind any one of us would drink. I didn't see any straws or glasses either. I watched Ram pour the opaque, pink milk into his mouth without touching his lips to the rim of the bottle. Then we waited by the road while Susheela tasted her mango juice. "Mummy, this is horrible," she said. "How can anybody drink it?"

Deshi finished it for her and spat on the ground.

The car started. We continued down the narrow road, past mile after mile of cane. The biggest town, in the midst of the cane, was Modiland — Modi Sugar, Modi Grain, Modi Machine Parts. "This man, Modi," Ram said, "is the third or fourth richest man in India."

"He's not the richest," Chotu said. "Tata is richer."

"Tata is richer," Ram agreed.

"Tata is a billionaire," Susheela offered.

"You cannot say he is a billionaire," Ram said. "I would say he is a multimillionaire. Isn't it, Deshi? Or have you forgotten India?"

Men in white pajamas peddled bicycles stacked with shivering sticks of cane past Modi Textiles, Modi Bicycles, Modi Fertilizer, Modi Saris and Ladies' Suits.

We stopped for lunch at what Ram called the halfway point, another open-air snack shop on the banks of a stagnant canal. Ram ordered fried potato patties, fried cheese, fried onions, and raw tomato sandwiches on crustless white bread. "We have the vegetarian," he said. "Now you must order your non veg."

The only nonvegetarian item on the menu was a deep-fried breaded mutton patty on a hot-dog roll. "I like vegetarian," I said.

"This cannot be," Ram said. "Americans like meat."

When the waiter brought the bill, Deshi and Ram reached for it at the same time. Deshi was faster, but Ram's arm was longer.

"C'mon, *yar*, let me pay for the food," Deshi argued.

"You are my guest," Ram said, shoving paper money into the waiter's hands.

"I can pay in dollars," Deshi said, waving his credit card.

"They don't take that here. Imagine trying to pay with a credit card for roadside snacks. What will the Americans do next? My God!"

"If I pay, it's foreign currency. We don't have to pay the luxury tax."

"Doesn't the tax on food and lodging go to help the poor?" I asked, an idea good enough to inspire me to take out my wad of rupees.

"Do you think the poor ever see that money?" Ram asked. "My God, Sally. How naive."

The car started. The road filled up with bicycles. Ram negotiated a path down the middle, like everyone else, then veered off to the left at the last minute, when cars, trucks, and scooters came toward us head-on. In the fields peacocks dragged their iridescent tails. In an hour we reached another town, both sides of the street lined with shops, carts, and hawkers fevered up with their last chance to sell before the night closed in. "This is Muzaffarnagar," Ram said.

"Very dangerous," said Sita, rolling up her window.

"Foo," said Ram. "Remember, Deshi? These Muhammadans. Knock just one of them off his bicycle, and he will pull you from the car."

"How can you tell they're Muslim?" I asked.

"By their dress," said Ram, "and just the way they look."

The men walking in the street, in white pajamas and long shirts, sometimes a little white cap, looked like anyone else I'd seen along the way. The women wore colorful Punjabi trousers and shawls, like Sita and Susheela.

We pulled up short behind a truck. All of us pitched forward. Glass tinkled down the bumper. "Oh, ho," Ram said.

"Papa, I was scared!" Susheela said. "Was everybody scared?"

"Pow," said Chotu. "I hope the driver is a Muslim."

The truck groaned into gear and pulled away. Deshi got out, squeezed between the car and bicycles tearing by, and looked at the Fiat's grill. "Did I hit him?" Ram asked.

Deshi made a circle with his thumb and forefinger.

We turned into a side street and stopped by an open-air booth full of wires, light bulbs, batteries, and glass, where another mechanic, his lips and teeth stained red with betel, wrenched the headlight off the car. He screwed in another bulb, forced a piece of glass on the light, and threw the bent rim in the window. Sita jumped. "Silly fellow."

Ram counted out some rupees.

By the time the car started again, it was dark. None of the bicycles rimming the asphalt had lights or even reflectors. Pajama legs glowed in the light of our new headlight. Susheela's head bobbed in the seat in front of me. I wished Chotu would fall asleep. He shifted constantly, knocking his knee against my thigh. One of the Reeboks Deshi and I had brought him had left tread marks on my shin. By the time he asked for the third time, I knew the Hindi for,

"How much longer before we get to the hotel, Daddy?"

I couldn't see anything beyond the shoulder of the road. Bullock carts loomed up in our lights, and Ram hit the brakes, leaning heavily on the horn every time. Chotu whined: "Daddy, how much longer . . . "

On the outskirts of Hardwar, the car climbed a hill, the first elevation since the Yamuna River bridge. Eucalyptus trees exhaled their menthol on the road. Beyond the trees, the ground fell off into impenetrable darkness. We climbed another hill. A row of lean-tos gave way to a stucco wall. A sign — Hotel Surprise — marked a gap in the wall. Past the wall another entrance opened in an iron fence. Ram pulled in. "This is it," he said. "Chotu, we are here."

"Hooray!" Chotu shouted.

"Hooray," his sister echoed sleepily.

Lurid paintings of women, their breasts bulging under sheer saris, lounged across a billboard on the roof of the boxy building.

"Oh, no," Ram said.

"This is a cinema," Sita said.

"This is a cinema, Daddy," said Chotu.

"Can we see the picture?" Susheela asked. "I haven't seen this one."

"Of course you cannot see the picture.

We have come to Hardwar to go to the temples, not the cinema." Ram backed out and asked a pedestrian for directions. The man pointed in the opposite direction.

We passed the Hotel Surprise again, and Ram said, "This is the hotel, isn't it?"

A tall, turbaned man in a white and gilt uniform, long mustaches waxed, obsequiously opened the Fiat's squeaky door. Ram got out. "This is not a five-star hotel," Susheela said.

"It is a three-star," said Ram. "There are no five-star hotels in all of Hardwar, Sally."

Chotu said, "I want to stay in a five-star."

"This is a three-star with five-star facilities," said Sita.

Deshi got out of the car. "Let's have a look at the rooms."

"Of course we will look at the rooms," Ram said. "I always look at the rooms."

The doorman wrenched open the back door. Chotu ran up the steps into the lobby. I crawled out of the car. My bones cracked. "I'm tired," I said.

"Sally is tired, isn't it?" Ram said.

"Everyone is tired," Sita assured me.

The lobby of the Hotel Surprise was paneled in marble and trimmed in brass, but the cracks between the white-gray slabs were not grouted. I followed Deshi up a wide white stairway.

The room was musty, with narrow double beds and red wall-to-wall carpeting. A fan dangled from the ceiling, its connecting wires visible between the fixture and the ceiling board. "What about heat?" Deshi said. The bellhop brought in a space heater and plugged it in.

"Okay," I said. I had no doubt it was the best hotel in Hardwar. Besides, I couldn't possibly have gotten into the car again.

Deshi and Ram went downstairs to check us in. I stayed in the room so I wouldn't have to watch them argue over who would pay. I was lying on the bed, almost asleep, when the telephone rang. It was Ram. "Will you have tea?"

"I'd rather have beer," I said.

"This hotel doesn't serve alcoholic beverages," he said. "This is a holy town. You cannot buy alcoholic beverages in all of Hardwar."

If I'd known that, we could have brought the two bottles of Haywards 5,000 we'd left in Delhi.

Deshi came up and I told him.

"How far is the next town?" he asked.

We were both asleep when the phone

rang again and Ram told us to meet him in the lobby: we had to see the prayers on the Ganges.

In the car, Chotu moaned next to me. "We have to get him medicine," Sita said. "His stomach pains."

"His stomach always pains," Susheela said. "I've never seen such a sensitive stomach on a boy."

"Someone should really stay at the hotel with him," I suggested.

"Oh, you must see the *puja*," Ram said.

I searched my purse for Kaopectate as we drove past increasing numbers of lean-tos, every third one lit with the blue glow of a television. People crowded the streets and pavements. Cows nibbled at the scraps in the gutters. The two-lane road narrowed into a city street lined with close-set buildings, their windows shuttered tight. Ram parked on an incline between two rows of dark, three-story buildings, and we walked downhill toward the Ganges. It stretched in the light of the moon clear into the night and cut so swiftly downstream that it seemed ready to take the dark town with it.

A bridge reached out to an island in the middle of the torrent, where temples seemed to have been dripped into cones and turrets like sand castles on a beach, their white marble lacework glowing in the moonlight.

"We missed *puja*," Sita said.

"We missed the *puja?*" Susheela cried. "Oh, no! How could we miss the *puja?*"

The marble steps leading down into the river were all but empty, the temples quiet and deserted. Only a few shops, selling incense and little brass figures of the gods, were open.

"Oh, you should have seen the *puja*," Ram said. "Thousands of people, singing and praying —"

"Thousands of little lights floating down the river," Sita said.

"It's so beautiful, Sally Auntie," Susheela said. "You should not have missed it."

Before I could remind her who had been driving, Ram shouted, "What are you doing? Sita, take Chotu's shoes! It is a temple, not a train station!"

"I am taking my shoes off," Chotu said.

"*Puja* is always at seven," Ram said.

At seven we had been checking into the hotel.

"We are too late, isn't it?" Ram said.

On the way back to the hotel, we tried three apothecaries for mint extract to settle Chotu's stomach. Finally we pulled up to an opening in a dark wall. A man in buff pajamas sat in the light surrounded by several burlap sacks of his exact shape and color. "*Pudina hah?*" Sita asked.

"*Hah*," the man said.

At dinner, back at the Hotel Surprise, Chotu took two drops of mint extract in a glass of water. When that didn't sweeten his stomach, he took two more. "Take a Maalox," Deshi said.

"What is Maalox?" Ram asked.

Deshi gave Chotu two antacids. He chewed one, his round face screwed into a grimace. Then he lay his head on his mother's lap, moaning while we ordered dinner.

"It's his own fault," Susheela said. "He eats too much candy."

"Why are you giving him candy?" Ram asked. "Sita, I told you not to give him candy."

We ate beans, infinitely harder on the digestion in my experience, and in the absence of beer, I settled for a fresh lime and soda, hold the salt and pepper. Then we went upstairs to sleep because it was nearly midnight, the television in our room didn't work, and the beds were half a length apart.

At three o'clock someone knocked on the door. "Who the hell is that?" I asked.

Deshi got up.

"You cannot open the door for your own sister?"

I heard the door open. "Chotu has a fever. None of us has slept."

From the bed I asked her, "How high? Do you have aspirin?"

"Do you have aspirin?" Deshi repeated.

"Have," Sita affirmed.

"How high?" I repeated. "Give him two. Every four hours. Get some soda — ginger ale is best — and let him sip it slow."

"*Dough asperine*," Deshi instructed. "Ginger ale, *hah*?"

"Ginger ale?"

"Any soda," Deshi said.

"Put a cool washcloth on his forehead," I said.

Deshi went across the hall to carry out my prescription. I fell asleep. In the morning, while I was drinking coffee brought up by a boy in livery, Deshi told me, "They had the entire staff in there, rubbing Chotu's temples. Ram's been crying."

"How long have they had this kid?" I asked. "Is it his first fever? You don't need a medical degree to know what to do for a fever."

While Deshi was taking a shower, I poked my head into his sister's room. All four of them were watching the only working television in the hotel. The sound track was playing a flute. A well-fed actor smiled as he held the flute to his face. On the holes his hands were still. "This is the story of Krishna, Sally Auntie," Susheela said, "the most famous incarnation of Lord Vishnu."

"Oi, Susheela," Ram said, "let your auntie watch."

I sat down on the edge of the bed. Susheela curled up under the covers to make room for me. Sita lay stretched out next to Chotu on the other bed. He looked a little pale, but he was sitting up, eating toast smeared with butter.

"We didn't sleep whole night," Ram said. "You should have seen us. I had everyone in the hotel fetching us thermometers, sodas, medicines. Even the doctor got up from his bed. Deshi got up. No one slept at all in this hotel, isn't it? Except you."

"We should take him back," I said.

"You must see the temples."

"We cannot go back," said Sita. "Doctor said that we must stabilize his temperature."

"It's already close to normal," I said.

"Is it?"

"You can tell by the way he's eating."

Sita pressed her palm to Chotu's forehead.

"First we go to the doctor's and pick up the medicine," Ram said. "Then we go back to

Harki-puri so that Sally can see Ganga in the daylight. Then we take a cable car to Mansa Devi —"

"You've been up all night," I said. "If we go anywhere, we should go back."

"If we leave by two," Ram said, "we'll reach Delhi by eight. Five hours to drive, one hour to eat —"

"We shouldn't even stop to eat," I said. "You get the medicine. Deshi and I can go to the temples by ourselves."

"But you are my guests."

"This is an emergency," I said. I looked out the window. At least the sun was shining. The wooded hills rose up against the blue sky, a relief after flat, brown Delhi. I couldn't wait to get outside.

I went back to our room while Deshi tried to convince Ram that we could get to the temples on our own. From our window I couldn't see anything — not the sky, the hills, not even the street two floors below. A thick fog had suddenly fallen. What would we see, I wondered, from a cable car on a hill above the Ganges?

Deshi rushed in. "The car won't start."

"No."

"The battery?" he wondered.

"The starter," I diagnosed.

In the parking lot, the car sat right where

Ram had parked it. While Deshi and I stood in the clammy fog, Ram walked through the gate with three men, none carrying tools. For half an hour they peered under the hood and clicked the key in the starter. Finally they walked the three blocks back to the garage. We waited. In another half hour they drove back, pushed the Fiat into line with their truck and stretched a pair of jumper cables from battery to battery. Ram turned the key: nothing.

Laughing they disconnected the jumper cables and drove the truck back to the garage. "It may be the starter," Ram suggested. Sita stood on the second-floor balcony, her shawl wrapped around her bathrobe. "What is Chotu's temperature?" Ram shouted. Sita went inside.

In forty-five minutes, all three of the mechanics walked back up the hotel drive. They pushed the car into the street, Ram at the wheel. Scooters sped by, bicycles. A cow lumbered past on the shoulder. Ram couldn't pop the clutch. Once, twice they tried. Then one of the mechanics took over the wheel, and the others pushed the Fiat until it rattled off to the garage.

"I have ordered the hotel taxi," Ram said.

"You go to the doctor," Deshi said. "We'll drop you and go to Mansa Devi."

"I must show you the temples," Ram said.

"You just take care of Chotu," I said.

"Besides," Deshi argued, "someone has to make sure they fix the car."

"I will take a scooter rickshaw back from the doctor's," Ram said, "give the medicine to Chotu, then pick up the car."

The doorman informed us that our taxi was ready, but the driver was still putting on his clothes, that as soon as he was dressed, he would take us to the doctor.

"My son needs medicine," Ram said.

We waited ten more minutes. Twenty. Susheela skipped downstairs in a red striped skirt and baggy sweater.

"What, are you out of bed?" her father asked.

"I'm not sick," she said. "Chotu is the one who's sick."

"Then you must care for your brother, isn't it?" he said. "Go. Tell Mummy to find out his temperature and call the desk with the exact degrees."

"Papa," Susheela whined.

"Go."

We waited half an hour, forty minutes. Sita rang in Chotu's temperature at 100. Fifteen minutes later Ram called back: 99. I asked Deshi why the garage still hadn't replaced the starter.

"They don't replace it," Deshi said. "They wind a new coil and put the old one back."

"Impossible!"

"That taxi driver must be watching *The Ramayana*," Ram said. "You know, Sally, that show is so popular that when it comes on, no one goes anywhere. It is our great epic, my namesake, actually."

"I read somewhere," I said, "that some people say their prayers in front of the TV."

"Where did you read that? It is ridiculous. No one does *puja* in front of the telly."

"What was that story about the Sikhs," I asked Deshi, "throwing money at a religious movie?"

"*A Ship Named Nanak*," Deshi remembered, smiling to himself.

"That's all right for the Sikhs," Ram said, "the Sikhs will do anything, but Hindus do not have *puja* in front of the telly."

By noon the fog seemed ready to lift. Patches of blue sky were winking through the clouds when the cab pulled up, complete with driver. Ram climbed in the front. "Dr. Verma," he said. We were not on the highway for a minute when Ram told the driver to pull into the garage.

After Ram had come back with the news

that the mechanics had begun working on the starter, the taxi took to the highway again. Finally we stopped in front of a storefront with a doctor's name written in Hindi, identical, in my ignorant eyes, to any other.

"This is not Dr. Verma," Ram said. "This is Dr. Sharma."

Deshi and I got out to walk. "Don't forget," Ram said. "You must take the cable car up to the top."

We walked along a cobblestone path lined with open-air booths, where men called out to us and held up plastic bags, each filled with puffed rice, a silvery garland, a marigold lei, two glass bangles, a sheet of those red felt dots that women wear on their foreheads, and a whole coconut. Deshi stopped at random and bought a bag. The hawkers shouted that one bag of offerings was not enough; we would need two.

The ticket booth for the cable car was closed, but the cable was still running, the gondola full of people riding down the hill. Deshi argued with the operator. "He said that even if we get a car to take us up, they'll stop it before we're ready to go down."

"Let's walk, please," I said. "They might go to lunch when we're halfway up."

The fog burned off completely as we

walked up a concrete stairway, then onto a winding path of stone. People short-cut up the gullies washed into the dry soil of the hillside. Cows picked their way up the steps. Packs of young men passed us laughing, arm in arm. Couples trudged by silently, not touching. I turned around. The Ganges stretched across half of its own valley, the size of a lake, rushing headlong to the sea. The last of the mist rose purple between the river and the hills on the other side, where I saw steps leading to a bare riverbed, like the ruins of a Roman amphitheater. This land still worships all its gods, it occurred to me, even the pagan spirit of this mighty river. "I wouldn't have missed this," I told Deshi.

"Even for the pleasure of a weekend without my brother-in-law?"

A few stucco buildings rose out of the crest of the hill. The temple of Mansa Devi was modest, painted yellow and red, with a few turrets and lattices, a marble floor, and an iron gate. Swastikas lined the crest of the wall. The way Deshi explained it, the Nazis got them backward. Stars of David framed the gates.

We checked our shoes, but the marble felt cold on our feet. "Keep your socks on," Deshi said.

Each little building held displays, some

in glass, some behind screens, of little porcelain gods, some dressed up in silks and gold like Indian brides, some with the faces of monkeys, the trunks of elephants. How did one see, I wondered, the divinity in these dolls? I backed away from worshipers bowing to these idols.

"What do we do with the bag of stuff?" I asked.

Deshi shrugged and asked a young man in a Western shirt and trousers, who was directing worshipers to a low hut where a holy man in a saffron robe with a long gray beard was opening the bags that worshippers had brought. He hastily poured out the contents into a pile in front of him, passing the coconut to a helper behind him. Then he scooped up a handful of rice, bangles, and dots and returned them to the bag. Deshi gave him our bag. He didn't even look at us. When he filled the bag again, he showed it to a porcelain doll in a red sari and gave it back.

"What do we do with this?" I asked Deshi.

"Give it to Sita. It's blessed."

We put our shoes back on and walked down the hill. The cable car had definitely stopped. Walking up and down that hill was the first time I'd felt in control of my fate all weekend.

Fifty feet down the hill a woman sat cross-legged on the path reciting prayers. She looked up and threw us a blessing. Deshi gave her a coin. The blessings followed us down the hill: "Good life," Deshi translated, "good family, good journey."

A man sat by the side of the path reading from a holy book. His voice rang out in a stentorian baritone. Deshi gave him a coin. He lifted his hand, not even pausing in his reading.

"In the beginning God created the heaven and the earth," I said.

The Ganges stretched out silver on the valley floor below, so wide Hardwar looked like an anthill next to it.

"The Spirit of God moved upon the face of the waters."

A woman at a bend in the path sat beside a huge brass jug. "*Pani*, sahib?"

We couldn't drink the water. Deshi gave her a coin, and she said something else.

"If we give her five," Deshi translated, "we can have the whole jug."

A few more holy hermits took our money, then the path led through a gate between two rows of lepers holding out the flesh and bone left on the stumps of their arms. As a doctor I was no longer shocked by this disease

45

I'd first read about in Bible stories. But I was still appalled that in a world that could transplant organs and microstitch nerves, these poor people still seemed to live like biblical outcasts. By the time we made it through the gauntlet to the street, I'd emptied my pockets.

My socks were wet. In the cab I took off my shoes and smelled something I had not smelled since I'd taken a course in large-animal biology. "Cow shit!" I said.

Deshi ripped off his socks. Our soles were black. Deshi paid the driver, and we rushed upstairs, holding our socks by the tops.

"Isn't cow shit holy?" I asked as Deshi and I sat on the edge of the bathtub scrubbing our feet.

Sita and Chotu were still lying on the bed across the hall. Ram was up and pacing. Susheela was watching another lurid television show. "We'll put Chotu in the back seat with Sita and Susheela," Ram said. "You and Deshi will have to sit in front. Five, six hours and we'll be in Delhi."

Sita took the bag of rice and ornaments and pressed it to Chotu's forehead.

Wedged in the front seat of the Fiat between Ram, who hadn't slept, and Deshi, who had the window because his legs were longer,

I sat terrified. High, boxy lorries rushed at us, their mawlike grills festooned with marigold-and-tinsel garlands. At fifty feet, the truckers took their lane and Ram took ours. I saw my face crisscrossed with scars, my head hanging by a thread. Ram broke for a bullock cart, leaned on the horn, and asked, "Sita, what is Chotu's temperature?"

"Papa," Susheela cried, "he's putting his feet in my face. Don't let him put his feet in my face."

"He must lie down," Ram said. "To keep his temperature stable. What is it, Sita?"

"99."

We stopped at the same restaurant. "Ram, *bhai*-sahib, there's no time," Deshi protested.

"We will eat in the car," Ram said.

"We cannot eat in the car," Susheela said. "Chotu will be tempted."

"He can probably eat something now," I said.

"I want a hamburger," said Chotu.

"Impossible!" said Ram. "Even if we weren't vegetarian."

At night headlights, always set on high, came at us head-on, yet passed miraculously, as if Lord Vishnu himself were riding on our hood.

Ram braked for unlit bullock carts, accelerated and passed, braked again.

"Sita, what is Chotu's temperature, please?"

"99."

Chotu giggled.

Fifteen minutes later Ram asked again.

"98.6."

"But that is low, isn't it?"

We bypassed Ghaziabad, which was a victory in itself. We crossed the Yamuna. Delhi welcomed us, so late that only the night watchmen pounded their staffs on the pavement as we passed the deserted halls of government, circled Connaught Circus and sped down Shankar Road.

"What about stopping at our house for some hot food?" Ram asked.

Deshi and I answered simultaneously, "No!"

"But your mother and your father won't be home. They spend every Saturday at your mother's sister's."

"We'll send Sitaram if we want anything," said Deshi.

"Even your servant won't be home," Ram said. "There is a big picture on the telly. He will be at your aunt's house too. Watching."

"What picture, Papa?" Susheela asked.

"We've done nothing this weekend, and now you tell me there is a picture on the telly?"

Ram didn't say another word. He pulled the Fiat up to the curb in front of Deshi's parents' bungalow, its whitewashed walls gleaming in the lights behind the low wall that surrounded the veranda.

"Take good care of Chotu," I told Sita. "Get some sleep."

"Hurry, Papa, the picture will be over," Susheela said.

Ram pulled our bag and coats out of the trunk. "I'm sorry," he said. "I wanted to take you to the temples."

"Forget it," Deshi said. "You did what you could."

"Ganga is beautiful, Sally, isn't it? I must go to Hardwar at least once a year." Ram's expression, drawn and drooping, caused Deshi to pat him on the arm. "You go through life day by day, but when you see such a beautiful place — and sacred, of God — somehow it all seems so much lighter — life, I mean. It's lighter."

"Thank you," I said. "Thanks for everything."

When the Fiat turned the corner, we sat down on the curb to wait for Sitaram, whom Ram would call, Deshi assured me, as soon as he'd told his mother what had happened, had his tea, checked Chotu's temperature, and remembered.

"It was a miserable trip," I said, unable to forget that vista of the Gangas. "Then he goes into a refrain about the beauty of the sacred or whatever it was."

"Just when you think you can't be any more annoyed," Deshi said, "he says something — what would you call it — redeeming?"

"Lighter," I said.

I looked down the dark, smoky street for the slim shadow of the family servant. The yellow light illuminated nothing but the tar and concrete of an ordinary, empty city street. I closed my eyes and saw Ram's Ganga again, her liquid hair laid out all the way to the Bay of Bengal in the bed of a holy river. No mere man could be reduced to the actions he took, the words he said. I opened my eyes. Same dark street, no Sitaram. Not even a pariah dog or a sacred cow. Still, there was something.

➤The White-Haired Girl◀

When I saw that white-haired girl opening the door of my son's New York flat, I lost my breath — all of it, as if someone had hit me in the stomach.

"Hello, Mataji," she said, as if I were her own, white mother, and she tried to kiss me with her bleached-out lips. She even tried to kiss my husband, the brazen slut, and she called him Darji, as if she had any idea what to call a proud Sikh. She tried to kiss Hermeet too, but he slipped away, laughing, as if throwing herself at men was some kind of joke.

That's when I said, "It's all right to make friends, but in India, your friends were not so ugly."

"Are you kidding?" he said. "This girl is a natural blonde. She's tall. She could be a model if she weren't so good with computers."

The girl asked, "What did she say?"

My son has been pressing me to learn English. But even my sister, whose own son, Deshi, also lives in America, will not study

English. We're too old. Our husbands speak it. Before the British quit India, they worked for them. Then came the partition, and we had to leave the Punjab. In Delhi everyone was speaking Hindi. But I have never had to learn a language to satisfy the men in power, and I never will.

I understand well enough. I understood the girl when she said, "Oh, come on, Hermie. I bet she asked you if I ever shit. Right? You told me your grandmother always said that white women never shit. Did she? Hermie, did she?"

I told my son to tell this girl my mother was the wife of a landlord, very rich. She did not have to concern herself with white girls' droppings.

"Keep it clean, Goodie-goodie," my son said, and, in our own sweet language, "What will you have to drink?"

"We will get our own food and drink," I said. "We are in our own home."

We had asked him, nicely, why go to the expense of two flats? He worked in New York, so he stayed in this flat during the week. On the weekends, he lived with me and his father in New Jersey. How could we take care of him, I'd asked, when he slept in New York from Monday to Friday? We would have preferred New York. We cannot drive. In New Jersey we could not walk to the shops. He said that this flat was too small, just one room and a kitchen. Now I could see: it was not small enough.

I sat on a mattress rolled into the shape of a divan. What would my sister think? She was older than me and wiser, though she had let her only son marry an American. I could not let this girl have my Hermeet. My poor sister bought that Sally the best Benarsi sari she could find and a proper set of gold jewelry. But the girl gives her only fourteen-carat gold, coats too heavy to wear, boots that make her feet sweat, and fabrics far too thick to be stitched into our fashions.

The girl was wearing a pair of jeans with half the color gone, just the kind I throw into the dustbin when I find them in my son's laundry, and a shirt open so far that I could see she had nothing on her chest. She was so tall that she looked more like a boy than a girl, though her pants were so tight I could see she had no fruit between her legs either. I wanted to weep for my son, but there wasn't time. When he followed her into the kitchen, I told my husband, "We cannot let this girl blind our Hermeet the way Deshi has been blinded."

"We must do our duty by our son," he said.

"Forget our duty," I said. "Think! My

sister's husband has a cousin who has sent his daughter to college in this country. We will call her father and invite them to Deshi's house. When Hermeet sees how rich this girl is, he will give up the white-haired girl."

On Monday after Hermeet left for the city, I called India. The girl's father was traditional, though he had sent his daughter to the United States. He wanted her to marry a Sikh boy settled here. He had refused more than one family on the grounds that the boys had cut their hair. That was a factor in our favor: our Hermeet still had his beard and turban, though he did shave a little. They would not see that in the photo I had paid a photographer to fix — wide mustaches turned up at the ends, beard beneath the chin. Their daughter, on the other hand, had already refused several proud Sikhs because she thought their turbans and beards were ugly. She could not refuse Hermeet. He was nicely featured, tall, very fair. I had heard that the girl was tall.

"She is tall," her father said, on the telephone from Chandigarh. "What is your son's immigration status?"

"He has not only received his green card," I informed him, "he has sponsored us all. He is very successful, American in business, Indian at home. Your daughter will have the best of everything — two flats, fully furnished, a handsome, successful husband, and, if I may say, a mother-in-law who does not interfere."

"I have no questions about you or the family," the girl's father said. "But so many of our boys have married Americans. Is your boy literally free? Has he had affairs?"

"I assure you," I said, "he is a simple boy. He prefers his own kind. He has his family in New Jersey. Every weekend he is meeting with his cousin-brother, my own sister's son, Deshi, who has begged me to invite you to his house. My nephew's house is your house; we will bring our son to meet you there. And this time next year, we will all be family — together."

My sister said she would not lie to her husband's family. "Hermeet is living with that American girl in his New York flat."

"He lives with his mother and father," I said, "like a proper son. He only stays in that flat when he works."

"Call me for the wedding. I will bring the sari."

"You will not have to bring my son's wife a marriage sari," I said. "Her father is so rich, he will give her ten pure silk brocades."

When the girl's father called from Michigan, where the girl had graduated, I wrote the number of the flight and the time of its arrival and called my sister's son to tell him family was coming.

"Who?" Deshi asked.

"Sardar Singh Singhia," I said. "Your father's cousin-brother, from Chandigarh."

"Have I ever seen him?"

"If only your mother would come back from India! She would be able to tell you who your own relative is."

"What's he look like?"

"He looks like your own father."

"And Hermie can't pick him up at the airport?"

"He is coming to stay with you. You are his family. How would it look if my son picked him up?"

"Yes, but JFK's so far, and Hermie works in the city."

Deshi is my own sister's boy, but I must say, he is difficult, always trying to avoid family obligations. It's the fault of that girl he married. When my sister lives with them Sally is never in the home to take my sister shopping. Sally has had no children. I don't even think she cooks for Deshi.

I called my son and told him that my sister's family was coming, that he had to come home to New Jersey right away.

"Why is it so important for me to meet Deshi's father's cousin?"

"Have you no feeling for your family? Have you lived in America so long that you can't extend your hospitality to Indians who have just come? How will I show my face to my sister if —"

"Okay, okay," he said.

"This is only family," I said. "It is a private affair. Singhia is very traditional. He has not come to meet any friends."

"What's going on?"

"A simple dinner."

I called Deshi again and told him that under no circumstances was he to tell Hermeet that an Indian girl was coming.

"First I'll have to tell Sally that you're planning a dinner at our house," he said.

"Tell her not to serve beef. The father is traditional. They have blind wealth. They are used to the best."

When Hermeet came home from the city, he took off his suit, though I asked him nicely not to wear jeans and a faded T-shirt to Deshi's house. He drove us half the way without saying one word; then he said, "Why are you bringing girls to meet me without my consent?"

"What is wrong with girls?" I asked. "I never knew you had any objection to girls."

"Why do you have to disappoint Deshi's cousins," Hermeet asked, "when you know I'm not interested in marrying anyone?"

"What is to be done?" I asked. "The family is here."

What to do — I would have to eat at my nephew's house. What would the girl's family think if the boy's mother refused food in front of her? But after this dinner, I decided: I would not touch a piece of food in the presence of my son until he agreed to be married.

At Deshi's house we walked to the door together, like the proper Indian family this girl would get if my son would listen to reason. Sally opened the door. Unlike Deshi, she had not cut her hair since she had married into the family. It was a pleasing brown color, but she wore it loose, like a young girl.

The Singhias were standing behind her. "So big you have grown," Singhia said. He was a tall, proud Sikh, his beard pressed nicely underneath his chin, his stomach big and healthy. "You will not recognize our little Muni."

The girl was standing next to her mother, not in our clothing but in an English frock, dull in color, cotton. At least her mother had the decency to see that the girl's legs were covered. Over her socks she was wearing two thick gold anklets.

"Such ankle bracelets," I said. "Are they gold?"

"Twenty-four carat," her mother said. "I brought them from India."

"Most girls wear only silver."

I wished my son would smile.

"How pretty she has grown!" I had to lie; there was nothing else to do. The girl was dark. And she needed slimming down, though no one could call her fat.

"And I understand your son is a big man in computers," said Singhia, as my son walked into the kitchen.

"Get me a drink," I heard him say.

Muni followed him. "I understand you're into computers."

"Software," he said.

"I love software. Where did you go to school?"

"New York."

"NYU?"

"Pace."

"I went to Michigan. I may go for an MBA at NYU. What do you think?"

"Go for it," he said. "What's cooking?"

"Goose," Sally said.

I hoped that Singhia would eat an English goose. I followed Deshi into the dining room, where Sally had sent him to lay out plates, like a servant. "Talk to my son," I said. "You are older. He respects you."

"May I help?" I heard Muni in the kitchen. "I can cook anything. Indian. American. Whatever you like."

"Can you bake a cherry pie?" Sally asked.

"I know the girl is not beautiful," I whispered to Deshi, "but she comes from a good family. Did you see the gold on her legs? When your Bombay cousins were married, the girls were not half so rich, and my brother's wife got five gold sets, two silk saris, a pashmina shawl, even a pair of shoes from Italy. I tell you, if Hermeet refuses this girl, we will never find one half so good."

"You haven't told her Hermie's interested, have you?"

"Of course I have. Look at him. He's twenty-three!"

"He may not want to get married."

"He does not know what he wants. You know how these boys are. One day he is going out with friends, and the next day he's leading some girl around our holy book."

We ate chicken after all, but Sally's food is always so bland that we have to mix it with hot pickle that we bring. Muni and my son were shy with each other, didn't say a word except, "Would you like more chicken?" "Can I have the bread?" and "Very good, Sally." They had the same social graces, these children. They were perfect for each other.

Before we left, Singhia's wife sat beside me and whispered, "Tell me truthfully. Is the boy interested?"

I took her hand and patted it. "Of course."

"We are going to California tomorrow," she said, "to look at another boy. It is only sensible, since we have come so far."

"You need not waste your money," I said. "We can make the marriage anytime you like. In India or here, where you like."

"Be patient," she said. "Muni is only just graduated. We will travel. Then we will talk."

Our son said nothing, only, "I hope you're satisfied."

"Such a perfect girl," I said. "Western-ized. Did you see how she was dressed? And her gold: Singhias are the richest Sikhs in Chandigarh. It's a wonder my nephews in Bombay didn't get her. But, of course, she will stay here. She is already adjusted to America. She will be happy."

"I hope she will," Hermeet said. "Now please, don't bring me any more girls."

A few weeks passed, and my sister told me that Muni had gone back to India engaged to the Sikh boy she had met in California. I was sick. I almost called Singhia to tell him that we'd take the girl without a dowry and pay for her saris, her jewelry, the wedding, even her MBA, whatever she wanted. My sister told me there was nothing I could do, that my son was as good as married to the white-haired girl.

It wasn't long before he started bringing her home.

"Have you no shame?" I said. They were sharing the same room like a husband and a wife.

"I'd say you had enough shame for the whole family," Hermeet said.

"We don't like girls living with you out of wedlock," his father said.

"Well, I guess I'll have to marry her."

I dropped his breakfast on the floor. "We know nothing of her family!"

"Do you have to meet them?" my son asked.

"We are the boy's family," his father said. "It is our duty to command!"

The next weekend Hermeet came home with four tickets to North Dakota. "If you don't go," he said, "Goodie and I will go without you."

His father had to carry me onto the plane, and then I had to fan his face with the emergency card for the whole trip, but we flew to that cold place, already covered with snow, and the girl's father met us at the airport. Such an ugly, red-faced man! The new white hair of age mixed with the old white stuff he was born with. The mother looked like the daughter: no chest at all, tall as a man. How she had ever given birth, even to a daughter, I would never understand. The house was good, that much I could say, with expensive figurines, a TV as large as a cinema, and wall-to-wall carpet in every room, including the kitchen. The moment we arrived, the white-haired man took the girl and my son outside and started up some kind of scooter with skis, and off they went across the snow. My heart stopped beating.

"The kids are off having fun," he said. "Now we can have our little talk."

They said they loved our son from the moment they first met him — they had stayed in his flat in New York, and we were not even consulted! They said the girl had never brought home such a successful boy.

"She has brought home other boys," I said into my *chuni*.

They were hoping for a wedding in June, but the girl didn't want to wait that long.

"We should be making the plans," I told my husband. "We are the boy's family."

The girl's father talked so much that my

husband, even if he'd been a stronger man, did not have a chance to open his mouth.

"Now. We would love for this wedding to take place in India," her father said, "but there's a problem. All four of us would have to get off work, and that's impossible. We're in retail, and this time of the year is deadly. Then there's the expense. We can get off for a long weekend in January, so we're willing to compromise and have the wedding in New Jersey. I'll pay for everything, except the ring, of course. And we'll be leaving just as soon as they go on their honeymoon. I understand they're thinking of the islands. Ever been there? Oh, the Caribbean's beautiful, and full of Indians."

"Go out," I whispered to my husband, watching through the window. That white-haired girl was rubbing the stuff in my son's face, laughing, her face as pink as my *chuni*. "Stop them! She's trying to suffocate him."

"It is cold," my husband said.

Well, we married that girl. My sister came back from India, and my daughter, Bubbly, came from Houston, where she had settled with her husband. My sister brought an extra-wide sari and a blouse stitched to the girl's measurements. Since she didn't have a sister — or even an Indian friend — who could show her how to tie a sari

(Sally always pleated her saris wrong), Bubbly had to dress her.

"Why did that stupid tailor stitch such a tight party blouse for a religious ceremony?" I asked. "She's sticking out all over."

"He must have got the measurements wrong," Bubbly said.

It was the first I noticed the girl could stick out at all. The skin on her stomach, between the blouse and her petticoat, was so white it made me sick, like the fat of an uncooked chicken, and she was not as thin as I had thought. There was no question about it: while I had been refusing food in the presence of my son, the girl had been putting on weight.

Bubbly wrapped the sari around her.

"Spread the pleats out on the belly," my sister said.

"It's a thick fabric," I said.

"Yes," my sister said. "It's thick." As she slipped her present, a gold chain, around the girl's neck, I heard her whisper, "Have children right away. Don't wait, like Sally."

"What did she say?" the girl asked.

"Yeah, what did my mother-in-law say about me?" Sally asked.

Bubbly translated. Sally frowned. The girl laughed.

"No shame," I whispered.

My sister whispered back: "When will you stop covering your face with your *chuni?* Any fool can see: the girl has been making arrangements."

"When we were this girl's age we could not even show our faces to our own father," I said.

"You are not even living in that country anymore," she said.

"How will I show my face in India?"

"You will say that the girl delivered early. In India they know: in this country there is no risk."

My sister was wise. Besides, my son would get a child at least six months before my sister's son and his wife. My sister said, "If it is less than six, seven months from now —"

"We'll call the priest again," I said. "And we will call the birth a miracle!"

➤ Gudrun's Saga ◀

If Hermie's parents ever found out that I'd been married before, they might starve themselves to death, the way they made a show of hunger striking when Hermie told them he was going to marry me. If they had any idea I'd been married twice, they might even try to kill me, though at this point I'm carrying their second grandchild, and even the first one was a boy. If they knew I was once married to a Muslim, they might try to kill Hermie for marrying me, though they could always tell themselves he didn't know.

He knew. I told him. After a year with Lars in North Dakota, I trekked out to California, flowers in my hair. The sixties were over, but not by much. I got a job selling furniture and hung out with the salesgirls. One night they sold me on a bar with live music and decent beer.

How was I to know the entertainment would be sing-along? There I was, towering over half the men, as usual, too Norwegian and too depressed to try even a single turaluralura, when I spotted him, my size, the best looking man I'd seen since I'd moved out on Lars.

I watched him for a good long time. He was sitting at a table full of mixed couples, Asian guys and American girls. Now that was something I had not seen much of in North Dakota! I pulled a chair up to his table. "Gudrun Sorenson," I said.

"Hashish Iqbal," he said. "Don't say it. I've heard them all."

"What are you?"

"Graduate student."

"Nationality, I mean."

"Pakistani at the moment. What are you?"

"Norwegian."

The crowd was singing "Irish Eyes" so loud that we couldn't talk, so we walked all the way from Geary to the Embarcadero, then back up the hill and clear across Chinatown. He'd learned the Irish songs from Christian Brothers in Lahore; I had sung them every St. Paddy's Day in Bismarck. I told him about the year I'd spent in Norway living with my cousins and a herd of cows, how I'd felt more authentic speaking my parents' language, even with strangers, than I'd ever felt gossiping with girlfriends in North Dakota. All of a sudden Hash and I were kiss-

ing, and before I knew it, we were at my apartment. Hash was damned near irresistible: there
was something dark about him, and it wasn't just
his color; after almost seven hours together, he
was still a mystery.

Hash's friends were anxious to get married, but none of the men could get up the nerve
to tell their parents. One guy went home to
India and came back with a wife. Arranged. I
couldn't understand that. My parents had been
dying to get me married ever since I'd dropped
out of college. They'd been devastated when
I'd broken up with Lars. When they came out
for Christmas, I introduced them to Hash. My
mother asked me what she and Dad should call
him.

"Hash," I said. "It means 'green fields.' "

"That's not what I mean."

"Boyfriend," I said.

"My dear, those men can marry twice."

"I wouldn't go out with him," I told her,
"if he had even another girlfriend."

She liked that. I was an only child. In
the absence of a son, my father had taught me
how to change tires, replace fuses, fix plumbing,
caulk windows. It had been my idea to go to
college, my idea to drop out when I realized I'd
rather be making money than grades, my idea
to spend a year in Norway, to move in with

Lars, then to move out when I realized he wasn't going to marry me.

Hash finished his degree and found a job. I couldn't stand the owner of the store where I worked, another in a long line of know-it-alls. Hash said I should quit. He'd pay the bills.

What was the point of having two apartments anyway? Most of his friends were living together, for want of permanent arrangements. I rarely heard from Lars, and when I called him, we talked as if he were the brother I'd never had.

Hash didn't have much stuff — a few pairs of jeans, T-shirts, and the blue suit he had interviewed in. He showed me a red silk outfit for Pakistani brides. "Gorgeous," I said. "What are you doing with this?"

The pajamas were a little short, but the shirt had lots of room. I wore it everywhere, to parties, even on the street. I felt liberated. After the demands of college, then full-time work just to support myself, finally I had some time to think.

I read articles about Islam. It's not all that different from Christianity, if you leave out the New Testament. Allah is just like God, and Muhammad was their Jesus, though he was not the son of God. But Hash had no idea what he was missing by not eating ribs, bacon, moo-shoo pork, or my mother's roast. "You drink," I said. "Isn't that a little hypocritical?"

"Probably," he said.

And then his mother died. We got a call at three o'clock in the morning. It was the only time I saw Hash cry. He took one of my good white towels and spread it on the floor. Then he knelt, facing the Bay Bridge, and knocked his forehead on the floor. I left him alone. I was afraid that he would go back to Pakistan and come back with that wife my mother worried about.

Hash's praying didn't bother me. He did it, usually, while I was still asleep, and when I got up, the coffee was ready. I thought: we're already living together. We never got on each other's nerves. I talked; he listened. I guess I had a weakness for compliant men. But there were differences between Hash and Lars. For one thing, Hash paid the rent; he had a graduate degree and a job with Pacific Telephone for life, insurance, pension. We had plans for his money: Norway, the Orient Express, the Himalayas, carpets.

He wrote a letter to his brother asking for permission to marry me. I couldn't understand why a grown man needed his brother's approval, but at least his brother wrote back right away promising to come for the wedding.

My mother bought the dress: lace on

satin with little seed pearls, a six-foot train, and a veil attached to a little pearl tiara. I wanted to go to Hawaii or at least to Mexico for a honeymoon, but Hash wouldn't leave his brother's family alone in our apartment, even for a week.

"You figure it out," he said. "You come all the way from Pakistan to see your brother after three and a half years, and he goes off and leaves. Besides, they want us to take them to Disneyland."

"Disneyland? On our honeymoon?"

"I'll owe you one."

"When? You're taking your vacation to get married!"

"I'll get another vacation after the first of the year."

"You've got to get a better job. They don't give you enough vacation."

"I like my job."

It was the first fight we'd ever had. I let him win. He promised we would go to Pakistan in January. I was dying to see marble palaces, reflecting pools, the highest mountains in the world.

I didn't meet Hash's family until just a few days before the wedding, when they flew to Bismarck, all four of them: Omar, Fakhri, and the kids. Fakhri wanted me to get married in the red pajamas.

"My mother wouldn't even consider off-white," I said.

"We wear white on holidays," she said. "And for funerals."

"Well, we wear black," I told her. "Red means you're looking for a man — the kind who pays."

Fakhri had brought me saris too, one black with silver, which I tried to put on right away, but I'm so tall that I couldn't tuck the edge into the slip and still have enough to cover my ankles. She laughed. "The tailor will sew a piece of gauze onto the border."

She gave me jewelry. It almost knocked me over: a necklace as big as a collar and shoulder-length earrings, twenty-four-carat gold studded with rubies. "You'll have to get the earrings converted," my mother said.

"I'll get my ears pierced," I said.

"But you know," my mother said, "in Norway, it's not done."

"I'll do it," Fakhri said. "I pierced Jaleela's when she was just a baby, and she didn't even cry."

I looked at Fakhri's daughter, thin gold rings glittering against her fat dark braids. They glowed so yellow that it made me hungry, though I thought six a little young for earrings.

I waited until my mother went out. Then I helped Fakhri sterilize a hat pin in boiling water. She held an ice cube to my earlobe. When the pin cooled, she pushed it through. Tears rolled down my face.

"It can't be paining," she said, "the earlobe is frozen."

"That's not it," I said.

She fixed one of Jaleela's earrings in the hole. I looked at myself in the mirror.

"The big ones will look beautiful against your white neck," she said.

I don't know what it was. I couldn't eat. By the time my mother got home, I was sobbing. All I could think about was a gypsy in Oslo who had read my palm.

Hash was annoyed. "It's just a little hole in your ear."

That was the last he noticed me. He spent hours listening to his brother — ten years older, potbellied, and bald, an ugly thin mustache. Omar insisted on carrying on these conversations in Urdu. "What are they going on about?" I asked Fakhri.

"They are planning the ceremony."

"It's all planned."

Finally Hash told me that they were getting someone from a mosque in Bismarck. I wanted to help them find a mosque, but Hash said it was a job for men. I thought the least he could do was let me meet his priest, since my minister had counseled us.

Hash hadn't said anything, even while Reverend Bergman ran through a barrage of questions about our compatibility, our understanding of each other's cultures, our willingness to respect each other's differences. I guess I talked enough for both of us. "I have never argued with this man. He puts up with my mouth, my laziness, even my lousy housekeeping. In return, I put up with his taste in food, his newspapers all afternoon, and what else? Right now his noisy niece and nephew, but they're leaving after Disneyland. As for differences in culture, we both sing Irish songs; Hash speaks better English than I do. His friends say he's more American than I. As for the rest of our lives, that's too much to think about. Right, Hash?"

"Have you given any thought to the religious instruction of your children?" Reverend Bergman asked.

I felt a jolt of panic. I looked at Hash. He hadn't reacted, just sat there with the same blank expression as when his brother was talking to him. "I can't marry you," I said.

"What?"

"Kids."

"What do kids have to do with it?"

"Weren't you listening? I've never thought about kids."

"We don't have any kids," he said. "Why worry about them? Why think about anything before it happens?"

Maybe he was right. The Muslim ceremony, after all the trouble finding a man to show up and read the Koran, took less than five minutes. Then he read the terms of our marriage. The $5,000 check my parents gave us, toward a down payment on a house, counted as my dowry, and Hash promised me the same amount as a traditional maintenance fee, if he should ever decide he wanted a divorce.

We were already married, in Islam, when Reverend Bergman began the service. His sermon concerned the Pilgrims and religious tolerance, a good choice, I thought, though the Pilgrims were hardly Lutheran, and the Indians were Native Americans.

The reception was a big, grand party. Hash's Indian friends were there with their American girlfriends, still waiting for the courage to get married. Lars had been invited too. I danced with him, and he told me that his parents were sending him to Norway.

"Wait a minute," I said. "You used to say you'd rather have a steak than a Swedish meatball any day of the week, that the Grateful Dead has got to mean more to us than Swedish fiddle music."

"Nothing to hold me here."

We took Omar and the kids to Disneyland. We shopped. I had my earrings converted to clip-ons I was afraid to wear. The stones were only glass, the jeweler told me, but the gold was real. Fakhri bought clothing, dishes, sheets, blankets, charging everything on Hash's card. During one of these trips, she told me she would come back to help me when I had a child. I told her about my misgivings. "Allah will provide," she said. "I will teach you how to raise a child, according to our ways."

Even after Hash had driven his brother and sister-in-law to the airport, I can't say we had anything remotely. resembling a honeymoon. All of a sudden I was the one making the moves. Hash had never been entirely uninhibited, but he had enjoyed himself, and he'd enjoyed me enjoying myself. But after Omar and Fakhri had gone home, he'd get right out of bed and shut himself up in the bathroom. I could hear him swishing water repeatedly. "What *is* this?" I asked. "Sex is dirty now? You've got to wash me off?"

"Don't be ridiculous," he said. "I can't fall asleep if I'm all sticky."

I don't know what went wrong. Hash

could let himself go and satisfy me too if he was doing it with a mysterious, foreign Scandinavian woman. But with a wife, it was something to be done in the dark, quickly, for the man's pleasure. But it was hard to tell what Hash was feeling, because he refused to talk about it.

"What is it? I didn't bloody the sheet? Is that what's bothering you?"

"You don't have your period, do you?"

"I'm talking about virginity!" I said. "On our wedding night!"

"Why should that bother me?" He turned over and fell asleep.

With Lars I could always talk, I thought, so I began to tell him everything by letter. He called and said he was following the Dead to California. I told him that, as I was selling real estate, I could show him some apartments in the Bay Area.

He looked paler, thinner, his straight blond hair falling all the way to his shoulders. "You look like an absolute Viking," I told him, and I kissed him like a sister.

"You look like Brunhild," he said. I'd put on thirty pounds in the year of my marriage. I'd tried to lose it, but nothing worked. Dieting depressed me.

"What the hell," Lars said. "Let's go on

an old-fashioned road trip. We'll drink a little beer, hit the beach, whatever."

I told Hash the truth. I've always been honest. That's my best quality. "There's nothing sexual about it. I just want to get away. You never took me on a honeymoon. I want to get in touch with my Scandinavian past."

"Where does that leave me?"

"In the future," I said. But that didn't sound quite right. "I'm just not coping with Islam at the moment. How do you think I feel, your distant object in the harem?"

"What are you talking about?"

"You never talk. We don't make love the way we used to."

"We make love. You talk enough for both of us."

"What ever happened to the thrill," I asked, "the first time we made it, that Sunday morning after walking back from that Irish place?"

"Passion doesn't last," he said. "You think you're the only one with a past?"

I went with Lars. That weekend — Swedish beer and pastries, the sun on the Santa Barbara beach, Lars in the best hotel he'd ever sprung for — took me so far away from Hash that I could never get back. Lars and I decided to invoke my Islamic right to a divorce, on the grounds that Hash and I had married under false pretenses. I thought I had wanted a man as different from Norwegian men as I could get, when I had really wanted Lars to change; Hash must have thought he wanted an American wife, when what he really wanted was another man's wife he'd left in Pakistan. We had both been wrong. We weren't the last. Of all the couples Hash had introduced me to, only half ever made it to the altar. Half of those had already gotten divorced.

I gave Hash the jewelry and his ring, but he insisted that I keep the clothing Fakhri had brought. None of it could have fit any woman in Pakistan anyway. I don't wear the saris anymore. Hermie's mother would have freaked if she'd seen that I already had a sari. I used up my dowry and the matching money Hash gave me to buy a condominium with Lars in Santa Cruz.

That was a long time ago, before the hostage crisis, Salman Rushdie, and Benazir Bhutto, fifteen years before Operation Desert Storm. Lars and I got married — in native dress in Norway at the little village church near my cousins' house. In the pictures I've got locked away with that black sari, I swear we look like brother and sister. I saw an acupuncturist and had my ear stapled to lose weight. The hole that Fakhri pierced had healed long before. Then

I saw a fertility specialist. He gave me pills and shots, and when they didn't work, Lars and I tried — I should say the gynecologist tried — artificial insemination. Then Lars got cold feet and begged me not to have any kids. That's what ultimately broke us up.

I moved east to finish college and got a job in computers. That's where I met Hermie. I married him because he didn't bore me like Lars, because he is Punjabi like Hash — not Muslim, though — and more ambitious than both Hash and Lars put together. Hermie's an entrepreneur, a workaholic, a man of the eighties. He has the money to take me to those marble palaces, those mountains. As soon as I have this next baby. If Hermie can only find the time.

≫ Grace ≪

Grace met Surinder at a party in Philadelphia. He was one of the few people there who knew anything about design, perspective, the re-creation of life in two dimensions. She asked him if he'd care to see her paintings.

He liked her geometric heads, their crossed eyes and twisted lips. "I wanted to study photography," he said, "but we were middle class."

"We're middle class." Lower: her father worked the line at Campbell's Soup.

"In our family we cannot afford to study art." He'd come to America for graduate school, like his cousin Deshi.

"I can't support myself painting," Grace said. She was waiting tables, resenting every minute away from her easel, her feet aching, a constant ringing in her head. Living with a well-paid man made more sense than struggling to support herself. Surinder liked photography; he'd be willing to spend some of his salary on paints and canvases.

Her parents didn't approve of cohabitation, but they had spent all their lives avoiding conflict; they went out of their way not to mention marriage. "What is he," her mother asked, "a Hindu?"

Her father said, "At least he's not a Catholic."

When Surinder finished his degree, his parents and his sister wrote him letters asking him to come back and "settle down" with "a good girl of your own choice."

"That means they're finding me a wife," he said.

"Don't they know about me?"

"You? They'd be over here in a minute, trying to persuade me that I've been seduced, that you were only interested in my money."

"You have been seduced," she said, "and your money is keeping me out of the bar six nights a week."

"I can't go, anyway," he said. "Without a green card, immigration would never let me back."

They were married in City Hall, the statue of tolerant, immigrant William Penn standing over them. They didn't dare tell Deshi, though he'd married an American himself. They didn't even tell Grace's parents. Only after the marriage certificate had secured Surinder permanent residence in the United States did he write his mother and father, telling them that he was planning a trip to India, that he had met someone he very much respected, that he would like to bring her with him.

The first call came in a week: Surinder's mother was ill, he had to come right away; his father was weak, only God could say whether he would live to see his son again; his sister shouted so that Grace could hear her voice from across the room.

Surinder went to India without her. She couldn't paint, couldn't even draw until she got his call: come right away; he couldn't tell his parents they were already married, but they had agreed to a quick Sikh ceremony in New Delhi.

Days passed in the courtyard of Surinder's parents' house. His mother barked instructions while Surinder sat, hardly reacting, on a cot made out of ropes strung across a wooden frame. Grace could never talk to him alone; his sister would not leave her side, would not leave Grace's hand unheld unless Grace sat on it or hid it underneath her arm. Surinder's uncles came, their wives, their grown-up sons. Deshi's parents telegrammed with their congratulations. Surinder's sister wrapped one of her saris around Grace, rose silk embroidered with silver marigolds, and Grace stood before a crowd and heard a bearded priest say her name — "Ga-race Mad-i-son." Then she and Surinder walked four times around the holy book and stood under a shower of marigold petals, the same flowers used to decorate their bed, the only double in the house.

She woke up to Surinder's rhythmic breathing and smelled dung smoke drifting in from the streets. The urge to capture that smell in a cityscape got her up. She sketched the sunlight coloring the cement walls of the courtyard, but then her father-in-law sat down beside her. Her mother-in-law came to advise her to take her bath while there was still hot water. Surinder's sister leaned over her shoulder to admire each stroke. Grace finally slammed her pad closed, packed it in her suitcase, and began to count the days until she could re-create in peace the oranges and golds that she glimpsed on the streets of Delhi.

Back in Philadelphia, in the bigger and sunnier bedroom of their new two-bedroom apartment, Grace painted the evil eyes of peacock feathers, the stripes of the Bengal tiger. She framed the few batiks and Rajasthani paintings she'd bought. Then she started on a series of Philadelphia girls, their breasts bulging out of midriff tops.

Surinder left her alone, the only man

who had never tried to tell her what to paint. It was the most productive summer Grace had ever had.

In the fall his mother came. Bibiji cleaned the apartment every morning, stopping only to burst in on Grace with a handful of corner dust for her inspection. Every time Grace opened a tube of paint, Bibiji coughed loudly. Toward evening she banged pots in the kitchen.

Grace watched, speechless. Unlike Surinder's sister and father, his mother spoke no English, and Grace spoke no Punjabi. She could have studied it at Penn, which was close by, but she didn't want to take the time away from painting.

"When is your mother going home?" she asked. "Two months is a long time to visit."

"I can't tell her to leave," Surinder said. "In India a parent is always welcome."

"But this is not India."

"I'm her only son. She wants to make sure I'm well settled."

"Well, tell her. You're very well settled. She can go home and get on with her life."

"She will. She misses my father and my sister."

And she did, but only after her four-month visa had been extended for four more months.

Another summer, and Grace painted folds of fabric, cascading hair, the sun on russet skin. She and Surinder bought a house across the river in New Jersey and made love on the screened porch, waking to the songs of birds. "This is even better than last summer," Grace said, and she wished it could go on forever. But just as the nights were turning cold again, Bibiji came back, with Surinder's father.

"I cannot live alone," he said.

"What is he talking about?" Grace asked. "They live with your sister."

"He's retired," Surinder said. "His pension won't pay the taxes, let alone the bills, and in India, you don't take money from your daughter. People say you're stealing from her dowry."

"Your sister's forty years old!"

"They can't leave her there alone. They'll go back. Just give them four, five months."

"Four, five months!"

In the mornings after Surinder went to work, Grace's father-in-law joined her for coffee. Her mother-in-law wiped the table, scowling while her husband commented on the weather or recommended products he had seen advertised on television. One day Bibiji shouted from the family room, where she was on her hands and knees dusting the floor.

"Bibiji wants a baby," her father-in-law said, almost blushing.

"Isn't she a little old?" Grace asked.

He laughed. "Not hers," he said. "She is impatient for a grandson to carry on the name."

Grace told Surinder, "If I thought you wanted babies, I wouldn't have tied you down with me."

"What are you talking about?" he said. "I don't want babies."

"Well, your mother does."

"Of course she does. She has no other chance for grandchildren. And in India, sons are everything. Haven't you heard my aunt complaining about Sally and Deshi not having any kids?"

"I don't understand your aunt's language. Tell your mother if I had a baby, I'd never get any work done. Even now I can't concentrate on a simple sketch."

"You can do any thing you want," he said. "I've never told you what to do. Have I? Have I?"

She had to admit that he never had.

"It's only temporary, Grace. A few more months. I just don't want to hurt them."

She stuffed her ears with wax, couldn't hear even when Darji knocked on the door of the third bedroom, which Grace had turned into a studio. He would walk in and stand behind her, for how long she never knew. She'd turn and let out a little scream. "We have no milk, no eggs," he would say, and ask her what she was planning for dinner.

When Surinder came home, she cornered him in the bathroom. "They're not children. They can buy their own groceries."

"They can't drive. You know that."

"Teach them."

"Me teach my father how to drive? He never even drove in India."

"This is not India."

"They'll only be here for a few more months. If they need groceries, I can pick them up on the way home."

But Bibiji and Darji never asked Surinder to run errands for them. Darji said that Bibiji didn't want to worry him. Grace took them to her friend, Joel, a doctor she confided in when she was still supporting herself serving double scotches to medical students. Darji translated Bibiji's symptoms, then revealed his own muscle pains, fatigue, indigestion, confusion with the fast talk on the television.

"Get a little exercise," Joel said. "Your wife too. Walk at least an hour every day."

"We cannot walk," Darji said. "Our legs are weak."

Joel sent them out into the waiting room. "I could order tests," he told Grace, "but my suspicion is it's arthritis, lack of exercise, old age. And tests can be expensive. Do they have insurance?"

"I don't know." She felt like crying on Joel's shoulder. The urge to rub her face against his auburn stubble propelled her back into her Japanese subcompact. Her in-laws' presence — Darji on the seat beside her, his turban pressed against the roof, Bibiji in the back in her polyester pantaloons and 1940s dress — made her want to get out of the car and hang out with the Philadelphia boys loitering in their tight black pants and tank tops.

Grace had never been able to approach a conflict with anything more flammable than paint. But she had to make her in-laws a little less dependent. "Darji," she said, "why don't I enroll you in a driving school, so you can drive yourself wherever you want to go?"

"I cannot drive," he said. "My legs are too short!" The old man's eyes filled with tears, and he shouted, his voice breaking: "It is for the children to care for the old. What is time to them? We have little time left. How much trouble can it be for you to take your Bibiji and Darji to the shopping center so that we will have a round outside our paint-smelling house?"

Grace tore home and dropped them off in the driveway. Then she took off and screamed at the highway for two hours before she felt spent enough to come home. She found Darji and Bibiji watching a situation comedy with a laugh track so loud that she could hear it from the yard. "Hello, daughter!" Darji shouted. "Did you bring the milk? Potatoes? Cooking oil?"

She found Surinder in the bathroom. "Call your sister," she said. "Write a letter. Tell her that she has to take them back."

"Just let them get their green cards."

"Their what?"

"Not to stay. It's just so they can come back any time they want without being hassled by immigration."

"I'm not sure I want them to come back any time they want!"

"They won't," Surinder said. "They're bored. They're missing my sister. Do you think they like being so dependent?"

"I don't know what they like," Grace said. "Except for afternoon TV, shopping, and, oh yes, babies."

"It's hard for them," Surinder said. "Everyone they know is dying."

"It's hard for me," Grace said. "*I'm* dying —"

"Don't say that!"

"I'm dying, you're dying, we're all dying!"

He put his arms around her. "Don't even say it. If I ever lost you, I'd lose everything."

She wanted to believe it. His arms felt good. Even with his parents downstairs, he was sexy, dark like the Philadelphia boys, but different. He had a future.

It took him another month, but he finally wrote his sister. Paenji answered by telephone, collect: she had no money, no husband, no son to take care of her; she had rented the house to Uncleji, who had moved in with a woman of questionable morals; Surinder had three bedrooms, air conditioning; she threatened to commit suicide if she could not see her mother and father again.

They put her in the third bedroom. Grace moved her canvases to the basement. While she carried a still life of mangoes and chili peppers down the stairs, Surinder's sister stood in the doorway, apologizing: "Do not worry. When you start your family, I will sleep in the room with the baby. When he cries, I will bring him to you in the bed."

The track lights in the basement ruined

her colors. The dampness warped the canvases. She bought a dehumidifier. The noise helped drown out the TV, the floorboards groaning under Paenji's weight, Bibiji's shouting from the kitchen, but the smell of onions, spices, and simmering meat drifted down the stairs.

Grace was tracing a perfect jawline, dead set on re-creating the face in her mind.

Paenji knocked on the door. "Am I disturbing you?"

Grace clung to the image just behind her eyes.

"One second," Paenji said. "Mummy is afraid you'll ruin your eyes, so I have ground up almonds with milk. You must drink it. I will not disturb you. One second only."

It was hours before Grace could even think of that face again, and by then the jaw was ruined.

She sent résumés to every college and private school within a hundred-mile radius. With her portfolio, the few successes she had had in shows and galleries, she hoped to get at least one painting course. She accepted a low-paying part-time position teaching drawing.

"When you're working," Surinder said, "it won't be all that bad. You'll come home late, and they're all in bed by nine o'clock."

Grace saved her salary until she had enough to rent a studio in Philadelphia. She set her easel in front of a long, bare window overlooking the street, then went out and bought a mattress, sheets, a comforter, and two feather pillows. In the waning light of the afternoon, she made a cup of coffee and stared at her half-done portrait of a gray-faced man.

She called Surinder at work. "Move in with me," she said. "Let them have the house. We can go back to being lovers."

"I'd like to be irresponsible, but —"

"You can be anything you want. You used to say that."

"I meant it. I'll be getting six figures by the time I'm forty, and you'll have so many shows you'll have to hire someone —"

"I don't want to hire anyone," she said, sobbing.

After she hung up she unwrapped her palette and stroked a little paint on the canvas. Then she walked to Surinder's office. "Let's go home," he said. "They'll stay up all night if we don't come home." He looked as gray as the paints she had been pushing around.

"No," she said.

She threw her energy into teaching, spent too much time with her students, even though she couldn't wait to get home and work on her new series: gray, lugubrious faces, their eyes mere holes.

After three weeks, Surinder called. "You've got to come over."

"Are you alone?"

"They need to feel they tried to reconcile us. It's how things are done in India."

"This is *not* India!"

Rushing into the classroom one morning, she found Darji peering at a student's sketch. When he saw Grace, he took the turban off his head and placed it on the floor at her feet. Grace snatched it up and held it out to him. His thin hair wrapped in a bun on top of his head looked more naked than her model. "What are you doing?"

"I am elder of the family," he said. "I forbid you to divorce my son."

"Class canceled," Grace said.

Darji fell on his face in the threshold. "I have humbled myself," he said. "Witness: I have touched my daughter-in-law's feet!" Grace's students stared, clustered behind Darji.

She put off filing for divorce. She knew Surinder would be putting it off, too. She loved him. She always would. But she'd loved other men. She'd gotten over them. Such memories could be sweet, productive.

Then Paenji's letters started coming:

The Bride Wore Red

Darji was dying, Bibiji had lost ten years of her life; Surinder did not eat; he shouted at the family. Two months later: Darji was better but would never smile again; Bibiji was eating, but only small-small bites; Surinder had a wicked temper and would listen to no one. And finally: Surinder was cold, he'd been spoiled by too much love; if the family had found a husband for Paenji she would not have had to live on his charity.

Grace finished a portrait of a gray-faced man, abstractly outlined with a skeletal jaw, a hanging, startled mouth, and big, uncomprehending eyes. In the corner of the studio that she had turned into a rudimentary kitchen, she watched coffee materialize in her coffeemaker, feeling as if, with this little space that no one else trod, no one else dirtied, no one else cleaned, she owned the world. Pouring herself a cup, she unwrapped her paints and began to put the finishing touches on a new piece she liked even better than the man — two gray-white faces, women, with just a touch of yellow. Elongated, the figures stretched from crown to abdomen as if they were hanging from the skyline behind them. They wore the same wide-eyed stares as the man, but she'd managed to work a touch of comprehension into the women's eyes.

Someone knocked on the door. She held

her breath. Paenji stood in the hallway lugging two big bags. She dropped the suitcases and threw her fat arms around Grace. "Sister! We will not be alone."

"What is this?"

"All that I own in the world."

"I told you," Grace said. "Surinder and I are no longer together. There's no changing our minds."

"I know, sister. I am reconciled. Even Bibiji and Darji are reconciled. Oi! So many steps!"

Her big haunches spread out on Grace's mattress. "We need furniture, sister." From the mattress she could see the portrait. Its dual stare turned her face as pale as the paint. "You made that?"

"I haven't made it yet."

"I won't disturb you," Paenji said. "I'll unpack quietly. Like a little mouse."

Grace shook her head. "How can I make you understand?" She pulled a chair up next to Paenji. "Would you like a cup of tea?"

Paenji shook her head.

"Then listen, Paenji, please. I can't work when you're around. I can't work with anyone around. And I need to work, all the time, even if it's only in my head."

"Everyone works too hard in America."

Paenji stared at the portrait, her eyes glistening with tears.

"Shall I call you a cab?"

"I can manage," Paenji said.

After she left, Grace found herself not liking her work in progress nearly as much. She dialed Surinder's office. "Your sister was here. I think you should pay her back that dowry."

"What?"

"It wouldn't take much: her own apartment, driving lessons, and if you're feeling generous, a car, some employment counseling."

"Are you coming home?"

"I am home." Neither one of them hung up. "If your sister can stop by, I don't see why you can't."

"If I stop by," he said, "I'll be caught in the middle."

The lines of her portrait blurred in front of her. She tried a wash. By nightfall she had managed to blend the foreheads of the women into the cityscape behind them. They no longer stood out as distinctive figures, individuals, together; they were disappearing fast into the big, gray city. Still, the painting needed something. Grace opened a tube of primary red, put a dab of paint on the tip of her finger and touched a dot above each figure's eyes.

⇥ Bridgewater ⇤
Burning Ground

One thing Iqbal Singh could say about Americans, they were fast. By the time his wife woke him in the room for visitors, the nurses had already changed the sheets on his brother-in-law's bed. They wheeled Herpal Singh to the basement and took him away in a car built especially to carry the dead. Herpal's son, Hermeet, drove the family back to the house. The widow sat in the back between Iqbal's wife, who was her sister, and her daughter, Bubbly, who had come from Houston to see her father die. "He has left me with twenty years to live," the widow said.

"Forty," said Iqbal's wife. "If God wills."

Iqbal Singh, sitting in the front of the Mercedes rolling his beads between his fingers, asked Hermeet where they were to get the ice.

"We don't need ice," Hermeet said. "They don't use ice in this country."

"But the house is warm," said Iqbal.

"They're not taking him to the house," said Hermeet. "They're taking him to a big house with all of the equipment. We'll see him there."

The boy was cold. America had made him cold. "We must order food for the consolation," Iqbal said. "All of the friends and family must come, the neighbors. In India we hire extra servants."

"Do you have white sheets?" asked Iqbal's wife, whom everyone called Babhiji, sister-in-law, because she was the eldest sister, married to the eldest son. "We must cover the house with white."

"Where am I to buy a pure white Punjabi suit?" asked the widow.

"No one in the family expects you to wear white," said Babhiji. "Light, fawn colors will do, even prints. You can give your dark suits to me."

"She cannot give you her suits," said Iqbal Singh. "She should give them to her own daughter."

"Her daughter does not wear Indian clothes. This country steals the soul as well as the body."

"I cannot wear a suit to work," said Bubbly.

"Work, work, work," her mother said.

"I may be dead myself soon," Iqbal said. "You will not be able to wear colors either."

"You've been threatening to make me a widow for fifteen years. And still I cannot say one word to my own sister without your interference."

Iqbal had learned, in fifty years of marriage, that absence was the only way to escape his wife's sharp tongue. How was he to know when the family married him that his silent sixteen-year-old wife would come to talk so much? Even Herpal, so much younger than himself and married ten years later, had not known his wife before his father had arranged his marriage.

Babhiji and the widow stretched out on the floor of the drawing room of Hermeet's house and talked on the telephone for hours. Herpal's brothers could not come. The flight from India was long and expensive, and obtaining visas was not easy. Babhiji called her son, Deshi, who lived a forty-minute drive away. Her daughter-in-law picked up the phone. "Deshi's on his way to Tokyo. What's wrong?"

Babhiji gave the telephone to Iqbal, who spoke English. "Come right away," he said. "Everyone is here for the consolation."

"It's four o'clock in the morning," Sally said. "Can I talk to Goodie?"

"She is in her room," said Iqbal, "asleep, as if nothing happened."

Iqbal hung up the phone and remembered how Deshi had canceled all of his business trips when an American hospital had saved him from cancer not two years ago: "Even my daughters came," he said. "Every day. They told Sally, 'Do this and try this.' They would not let their father die."

"The day we took my husband to the hospital," the widow said, "he was shrieking, 'I won't go! I won't go!' He knew that he was never coming home."

"He wanted to die in India," said Iqbal.

"No one wants to die anywhere," said Babhiji. "If it had not been for India, he would not be dead."

The widow sobbed.

"It was the hepatitis," Iqbal said. "Sally said that he contracted hepatitis on a pilgrimage."

"No one can fall ill on a mission for God," Babhiji shouted.

"He was not boiling the water," Bubbly said. "He was eating at the roadside stalls."

"He would not have lived even for a month if my daughter had not gone to India and brought him here," said the widow, stroking Bubbly's back, her *chuni* crumpled in her hand.

"For nearly two years this country kept him alive," said Iqbal.

Babhiji said, "And all the time he begged his son, 'Send me back.' He never wanted to live in this country. He did not want to die here either."

"How is it so bad?" Iqbal wondered. He remembered how he had urged Herpal to come back to America.

Herpal had complained, "Our *gurdwara* so many miles away that our children cannot hear the words of God."

"Forget about the *gurdwara*," Iqbal had told him. "From India I have brought color pictures of every Sikh guru."

"In America our gurus are no more than pictures that our daughters-in-law will not have about the house."

"In our drawing room, we have one giant statue of Lord Siva."

"Your son-in-law's god of destruction is no more than a parlor ornament."

"We must do our duty by our children."

"I have done my duty."

"Our sons live in this country. It is our fate to live here with them."

"It is my fate to think of God. How am I to wash away my sins in water that runs swiftly from a tap?"

It had been Iqbal's duty, as Herpal's elder, as a man whose own son had married an

103

American, to give Herpal advice: "Do not expect this girl to cook your food every day. We cannot live as we have lived in India. On the other hand, it is not difficult to cook with an American stove."

Herpal shook his head. "I prefer the holy food of our own *gurdwara*."

"Our daughters-in-law cannot take us to the *gurdwara* every day."

"I will fast until my son's wedding feast. Then I will return to India."

Hermeet's mother had stayed in America; Herpal had gone back. Goodie gave birth to a son, then a daughter, before Herpal visited America again, after his health forced him to retire. He read his holy book from morning until evening, every day. Once when Iqbal took him on his daily walk, Herpal told him that in India a village priest had married a *peepul* tree to a *neem* tree.

"In America this grafting is a science," said Iqbal. "They make a peach with the skin of a plum."

"They wrapped a sari around one, a Brahmin's thread around the other."

"That is superstition," said Iqbal. "Trees cannot be married. They cannot even move."

"The priest carried the fire around them.

The spot is blessed. Good fortune will come to the village."

"We Sikhs don't believe in this Hindu superstition," said Iqbal.

"In India," said Herpal, "even the trees have souls."

If men's souls could transmigrate into vegetables, Iqbal thought, lying in the very room where Herpal had last slept before dying in an American hospital, Herpal's spirit might now be sprouting in some dusty village bazaar. All men must die, but in America, with morphine, local anesthesia and all such drugs, no man should have to suffer. Herpal had gasped for breath for thirteen hours. Religion says with every breath a dying man is counting one past life, Iqbal remembered. Sally had explained it scientifically: when the liver is no longer functioning, the poisons in the blood destroy the kidneys; the body fills with water; the breathing does not stop until the lungs are full.

Iqbal could not sleep. When a man is old, he realized, he must give up desire and listen to the yearnings of his soul. But Herpal had gone too far, in Iqbal's opinion, by taking up a begging bowl and walking into the forest like a holy man. He had a duty to his family. His wife was still alive. Even the holy book says you cannot find

God through pilgrimage. Iqbal had stayed with *his* family in the United States so that he might convince his son to have a child. For how can a man go to his grave without a grandson to carry on his name?

Iqbal must have been dreaming when he heard Herpal say, "Our lives are the dream, death our waking from illusion." For a moment Iqbal thought he was in the hospital again, before his wife had wakened him and told him that Herpal had breathed his last. Then he heard her calling him to have his bath; it was nine o'clock, and the family was going to the burning grounds.

At the house built especially for viewing the dead, a priest Hermeet had brought from the *gurdwara* said a prayer, then a man the family did not know, in a black suit like the Americans from Hermeet's business, closed the coffin and instructed the family to get into the car and turn on the lights, so that no one would break into their funeral procession. The Mercedes followed a big, black car down the main street of the town, then onto the freeway. Trucks passed them, cars pulled onto the road in front of them. Iqbal warned his nephew not to lose the black car. "He's only going forty," Hermeet said. "It's impossible to fall behind."

Hermeet left the highway and drove for

ten minutes past a shopping center, through a small jungle to another town. In the middle of the town was an iron fence and a big stone arch with a sign, "Bridgewater Memorial Park," at the top, but it was not a park; it was a cemetery, like the British cemeteries Iqbal had seen in India. They rode past little stone houses for the dead, statues with dirty wings, plain stones with the names inscribed on them, trees and shrubs, pots full of flowers. He would never understand how English ladies could take their walks in cemeteries.

The cars stopped at a small stone house on the other side of the cemetery, nowhere near a river, though Iqbal could see the highway clearly in the distance. The family followed the man in black through a door and down a ramp into a basement, where two large ovens sat on the concrete floor. Iqbal knew what they were. One of them was roaring, and they looked like the ovens of the restaurant where Deshi bought pizza. The widow shrieked. "Come," said Babhiji, "do you want to keep the body now that the soul has flown?"

A man in jeans pushed the coffin into the empty oven. The priest said prayers while the man in jeans stuffed the flowers in and closed the door.

"This is just like burial," said Iqbal.

"You can do what you want with the ashes," the man said. "Some bury them."

"The son must take them to our holy river," Iqbal said. "He must light the fire. When my father died, as I am the eldest, it was my duty. He was so high — on a pile of dry wood, covered with so many flowers. I was just a boy. My aunts and uncles had to push me. 'Touch the torch there,' they said, 'there. It must catch. Has it caught? Has it?' "

Hermeet put his finger on a red switch, like a light, and pushed it up. The oven started roaring. The widow fell into Babhiji's arms. "Gross," Goodie muttered as the children clung to her legs and cried.

One advantage of this American technology occurred to Iqbal: with such ovens it would have been impossible for a widow to jump into the fire to save herself from the lives to come. Still, he missed great tongues of flame darting into a parched New Delhi sky to lick the underwings of vultures and pariah kites. "When must we come back to gather the flowers?" he asked Hermeet.

"They deliver. The ashes, I mean."

"We must make a trip to the Ganges."

"Bubbly is going in August."

"A daughter cannot do it."

"Have you no shame?" said Babhiji. "For two years the man begged his son to take him back, and that son can't even take the time to carry his ashes to the Ganges?"

"Someone will take them," Hermeet said, patting Babhiji on the arm. But Iqbal was afraid: if the only sons could not take time to immerse their fathers' ashes in the holiest of rivers, the fates of the sons would not be kind — in the next life, if not in this.

Iqbal could still hear himself advising Herpal, after Bubbly brought him back that last time: "At least you must be comfortable. Who knows how many years you have? Thank God it is our fate to live in a house with the conveniences — warm air in the winter, cool air in the summer, one hundred varieties of bread, anything you want, and clean."

Iqbal had meant to make Herpal feel better. And he still believed that to extend one's life was good, that America had given him that much. But America had burnt Herpal like garbage in a basement furnace. "American convenience is the finest of illusions," Herpal had said. "Never be ashamed that it has filled your eyes."

Outside in the graveyard, flakes of snow had begun to turn the black car white. Iqbal felt a chill as he hurried toward Hermeet's Mercedes. Even he had come too far to see the gods of India, he realized, though in Deshi's drawing room Lord Siva still posed, frozen in a ring of fire.

❯❯ Doctor Doktor ❮❮

Siddharth Doktor welcomed the Punjabi lady into his office. By her wide trousers gathered at the ankles he recognized her culture and her language; he knew she was Sikh by her bun of dyed black hair and the steel bangle on her wrist.

"Gujarati," the lady muttered to the American who left her at the office door.

"You just go in by yourself, Mataji," the American woman said in English, returning to her four Anglo-Indian children, who were running around the waiting room tearing up the magazines. "He's Indian. He can talk to you."

"Yes, I'm Gujarati," Siddharth said. After twenty years in the United States, he was resigned to Americans' inability to distinguish Indian communities. He could not speak Punjabi, but he knew Hindi, and that was close enough.

"Mrs. Herpal Singh?" he asked, reading from the form that the American daughter-in-law had filled out for her.

"Bombay?" asked Mrs. Singh.

"Yes, I'm from Bombay."

"We live in Delhi. When we don't live here."

He could have told her what her problem was without listening to the litany of nervous symptoms he recorded on his pad: headaches, muscle spasms, dizziness, palpitations . . .

She told him she'd been in this country off and on for more than five years, since 1980, when her son had married, against her wishes, the woman in the waiting room. She had no other son, and this one was not going back, so she felt she had to live with him in America. She had become a widow not one year ago, here, in America, from a disease she had expected American medicine to cure.

"Against God and hepatitis we can only do so much," Siddharth interrupted.

She said she'd had little income even when her husband was alive. She was totally dependent on her son. Recently her son had moved from Long Valley, New Jersey to Portola Valley, California, so she could no longer spend time with her sister, who had lived not far away in Short Hills, New Jersey. Her sister did not have to consult a psychiatrist. *Her* husband was still alive. And *her* daughter-in-law was a doctor who did not insist that she must be crazy because she could not forget the husband she'd lost in the country that had been supposed to save him. Siddharth stopped taking notes while Mrs. Singh went on: no one was ever home in the suburbs where her son had settled; there was no one to stop by with a tip on a good buy on Kashmiri shawls or a new style of Punjabi suit. Even her daughter-in-law was too busy for her, and her son always took the girl's side.

Siddharth made a show of listening. It was not the sort of case that interested him. But all of his cases shared the same general problem: this Punjabi lady had been living a life ill suited to her identity. She was caught between two worlds. So was Siddharth.

It had not been entirely because his surname is Doktor that his family had decided to send him to medical school. Siddharth had not done well enough in math to be an engineer, but unlike the rest of the family, he had a better head for studies than for business. He had always been a dreamy boy, his sister said, quiet and thoughtful, like a poet. But no one could support a family on a poet's doles, his father said, and besides, the Doktors were not Brahmins to be coddled and fed for their knowledge. His mother thought it bad karma that no one in her husband's family had ever been intelligent enough to live up to his name.

But why psychiatry? Wasn't it enough, his father asked, to measure blood pressure and listen to the heart? His only son had to waste his time and the family money treating illnesses he could not see?

"People spend their lives pursuing what they cannot see," Siddharth said.

People who give up their possessions, abandon their families, and wander from temple to temple with only a loin cloth and a begging bowl, his mother said. But when the family heard that Americans paid millions to discuss their sex lives with strangers, they sent Siddharth to America.

They married him before he left, afraid that he might end up alone in a single room, his mother and sister several thousand miles across the world.

He was happy with his parents' choice. She would not disturb him at his research. From the very evening that Siddharth and his family had gone to meet her, Mina had sat silently. She sat quietly throughout the wedding ceremony and on entering the Doktor house, where they spent the first few days of their marriage. She broke the silence only after the long flight west, after they had moved into a one-bedroom apartment on the twelfth floor of a highrise for married students on the campus of Indiana

University, where Siddharth had won a fellowship to study human sexuality. Siddharth had been thrilled to find colleagues with enthusiasm for his interests. The library provided books he would have had to special order in India. But Mina had been disappointed that no one had stopped by to welcome them. Siddharth came home in the afternoons to find her sitting on the mattress in a fresh silk sari, staring out the window at the stadium across the parking lot. Every day she informed him, "I have not spoken to a soul from the time that you have left in the morning until the time that you have come home."

Siddharth tried to tell her how busy people were in America. He'd noticed right away that hourly breaks for tea just did not happen. He invited his colleagues and their families. Mina cooked a curry so hot that only one man from Korea could eat anything but rice and yogurt, the plain yogurt left over from the spicy side dish. Siddharth invited Indians that he identified in the corridors, the elevators, or the parking lot, foreign students, who sat on the pillows strewn across the carpet that Mina's family had sent, reminiscing about favorite restaurants in Bombay, Delhi, Karachi, and Lahore. Siddharth hadn't been in Indiana long enough to miss India, and besides, he had come to stay. But these dinners left Mina longing for the friends and family she'd left behind. "If my mother knew that I was serving dinner to Muhammadans, she would call me back."

"In America we cannot pick and choose," Siddharth said, "if we want our friends to be Indian."

Evening dinners could not keep Mina busy during the days, when their new friends worked, attended classes, or were busy with their children. Mina had no one to sympathize with her longing for the snacks and curries, the ice cream and specialty sweets, the shopping for saris and twenty-two-carat gold, the long, sunny mornings with her mother and sisters, the company that had never left her alone in India. Siddharth suggested that she take some courses.

She was through with school, she told him. She had come to America to make a doctor's house.

He suggested that she work until they could afford to buy a house and raise a child.

She reminded him that she could hardly keep a doctor's house if she was going to exhaust herself outside the home like a woman who could not find a husband to support her.

Siddharth brought work home. Mina made tea and chopped fruit, then sat next to

116

him and enumerated the spices she had mixed with the fruit. "I wish we could get proper Indian *chat*," she said. "My God, I miss that *chat!*"

"Mina," Siddharth said. "I can't concentrate when you're talking."

"What do you expect me to do? I've already scrubbed the apartment from top to bottom."

"Read a book. You were a literature major."

"I had enough of reading in college. I know! Why don't we play cards?"

"I'm working," he said. "I told you I would bring work home."

"You work too much. You'll hurt your eyes."

He asked Mina why she had married him, knowing that she would be coming to America.

"What a thing to ask!" she said. "You are a doctor. In America a doctor can make millions. And besides, you are my husband. I love you."

Eventually he came home to find Mina lying on the bed, with a headache, nausea, exhaustion. Psychosomatic, he decided, or perhaps the first signs of clinical depression. "Mina, darling," he would say. He would press her legs, and sometimes they'd make love. That would cheer them up, as his studies had shown it would, at least temporarily.

One afternoon she greeted him with the news that she was going home. "Mina, please," he said. "It's not so bad. I'm trying —"

"Every woman is entitled to return to her father's house to have the baby," she said.

"Baby?"

He would have liked to have children two, three years after he'd established himself in a practice, after he and Mina had enjoyed their lives a little, when he had completed the research that had drawn him to America. But he realized he had never mentioned family planning.

"You cannot go," he said. "What will I do?"

As it turned out, he could not afford to send her home on the money from his postdoctoral fellowship. The baby was born at Monroe County General. She was disappointed when the obstetrician identified it as a girl. "Why?" Siddharth asked. "In America it doesn't matter."

"Doesn't matter? A daughter will not care for us when we are old. She will have to care for her husband's parents. Only with a son is a mother sure that she will not be left alone when she is old."

"We're so young," he said. "Why are you so afraid of being alone?"

Mina's plan, he realized, was to save up a lot of money and then go home, but when Siddharth considered India, he remembered patients drugged to sleep in the corridors of the mental institution where he'd done his residency, families performing exorcisms over the insane that they had themselves, in Siddharth's opinion, driven crazy with their superstitions. He did not think that any Indian university would welcome his investigation of homosexuality. But so they could live in a larger Indian community, he left the institute. In San Jose, California, Mina gave birth to a son, not two years after Tara had been born. Then she would not rest until she'd had another.

Siddharth's practice thrived. Patients came from all over the Bay Area, some of them with genuine problems. Word had gotten around: Sid Doktor was not one of those old-fashioned shrinks who considered homosexuality an illness, but a genuine guru who understood how much it hurt to be an outcast in American society. Mina could easily have afforded a nanny.

"Why should I hire a stranger to raise my children?" Mina asked. "No one here can speak our language. In the kindergarten they pronounce our daughter's name like the house in that *Gone with the Wind*, and they call me Minah, like the bird. On the telephone your patients ask for Sid."

"God knows my patients have enough trouble without struggling to pronounce my name. Besides, you want to be accepted, don't you?"

"Perhaps it makes you feel less Indian to call your family by American names, but these Americans think we are Mexican."

"Most people think I'm Jewish."

"How can you live in a country that knows nothing of your culture?"

"That's not true. Some of my patients are fascinated with India. They have read the Bhagavad Gita and the Kamasutra. Have you read them?"

"Don't be disgusting. I studied Shakespeare."

After Tara started school, the Doktors could visit India only in the summer, when Bombay was so hot and humid that their shoes got moldy. Mina took the children every year. Siddharth could rarely find the time to join them until the last two weeks of August. He drove home from San Francisco International every June with an emptiness that restaurant meals and intercontinental phone calls could not fill.

But the years went by, winters in San Jose, summers in Bombay. Mina and the kids sweltered in the Indian heat and the monsoons and moped through the rain and fog of northern California. Eventually the contradiction got to Mina. "Bombay is beautiful all winter," she said. "San Jose is not so hot in the summer and not nearly as smelly."

The conversation, which had started in bed after a day of chilly drizzle in San Jose, culminated in Bombay on the veranda of the Doktors' bungalow, monsoon rain slashing through the palms that lined the busy street. Bare feet padded by, middle class men keeping their heads dry under wide black umbrellas. Siddharth's mother asked, "What sense does it make to send the children to India only during holidays when they could be attending the English medium school that prepared you so well?"

When would the children ever speak the family's Gujarati in America, Mina added, a language that would remind them who they were no matter where in the world they might live? Could Spanish I, II, and III do that?

Siddharth couldn't disagree with the importance of identity. And it was true what they said about the schools. He was the only doctor he knew who had learned how to express himself grammatically, and as the school he had attended had been rising academically, education in America had been slipping.

He lasted, by himself in California, until almost Christmas, which had always been a time for argument — the kids pressuring Mina into buying a tree, putting up lights, and exchanging gifts like their Christian classmates. She stopped short of the turkey dinner, since she had always been vegetarian and still resisted the hamburgers and hot dogs that the children loved. In his mind, Siddharth sat on his parents' veranda watching the warm rains of Bombay. Mina was bringing him tea. The kids were slapping cards down on the marble floor. His mother was preparing dinner, hot even to the smell, as his father hobbled home, leaning on his cane. Siddharth was able to join his family for the holidays. Mina was too busy with her social obligations to bring him tea, but servants brought him anything he wanted. The boys were always out, on the soccer field, at cricket. Tara was almost thirteen all of a sudden, and in just four months she had begun to look like a woman. "Why can't I play?" she cried. "I was on the team at home."

"This is your home," said Mina, standing at the door arranging her sari one last time before rushing through the drizzle to a waiting taxi. "Football is too rough for girls. Do you see any of your classmates playing it?"

"My classmates are all JAPs."

"Japs?"

"Well, GIPs, then: Gujarati Indian princesses."

"Watch your mouth, Tara," Siddharth said.

One day Mina brought Siddharth a magazine, the plump, ruddy face of a starlet on its cover. "You can make money here," she said. "You need only advertise. Haven't you seen the new billboard on Marine Drive? 'Having problems? Consult Dr. Patel, Sexologist.' Well, 'Consult Dr. Doktor. America returned. Psychiatrist of the stars.' "

"It's not true," Siddharth said.

"You are not America returned?" his mother asked.

"Mina, I can't. I haven't built up a practice in California to stay here and gossip with half-Westernized film stars —"

"Let's go home," said Tara. "I haven't seen a blond in six months!"

"Do you want her to marry a blond?" asked Mina.

"I don't care who she marries," said Siddharth, but he realized that it was his duty to make sure that Tara married well.

"I'm not getting married," Tara said.

Mina smiled. In India, her happiness could not be shaken.

Siddharth went back to California, but only to sell the house and refer his patients to his colleagues. He was back in Bombay before the next monsoon. With money from the San Jose house, he could open an office. But after several months he grew tired of looking for the right space and tired of wasting time at home, where his mother argued with his sister and his cousins, aunts, and uncles dropped by daily and stayed for hours discussing clothing, food, and parties. The talk had dulled his powers of listening; he needed the distance of a doctor-patient relationship to sharpen his skills again.

The real estate agent told him that if he wanted to move into an office, he'd have to pay double the rent that the landlord had asked for, in cash. Siddharth wanted to charge the landlord with extortion.

"You have forgotten the social graces," his mother told him. "If you would not talk about your private concerns, no one would know how you obtained an office."

"We should have come home sooner,"

Mina said. "The landlord is probably cheating you because you have become a dumb American."

"It is true," his father said. "I will go with you. If he doesn't take twenty-five percent, we will threaten to bring in the government inspector, who is the friend of my real cousin."

Siddharth felt as if he were ten years old. He missed his patients' stories of unrequited love, seductions, ill-fated affairs, and self-destructive crises. When he was in college, he had wondered what had been wrong with the handsome boy his parents had chosen for his sister. He was not a man, Siddharth's mother had whispered, so his sister had come home from her husband's house, while he had stayed with his parents in a closet darker and more tightly sealed than that of any of Siddharth's American patients. Siddharth had always regretted that no one had helped his poor brother-in-law see himself for what he was — not as others saw him. He recognized a similar need in himself.

"You had better keep up a supply of placebos," his friend Ashok suggested. "These days even the gurus are giving herbal remedies. You know how it is in India: if you can eat it, it is much better than to have to talk. Silence is the only privacy we have. But enough about India! What kind of car did you drive in America? How much did you pay for petrol? Why did you ever leave?"

Ashok provided Siddharth with his first patient — a newlywed who, like Siddharth's sister's husband, had found himself impotent. "I've checked him out," Ashok said, "and I can't find anything physically wrong. His parents are broad-minded; they asked me if he needs a sexologist. Traditional parents blame the wife."

The young man had brought his wife into a house occupied by his brother and sister-in-law and their three children, his mother and father, a widowed aunt, and an old man unidentifiable as a relative, though he had been in the family since the mother and father had married. Siddharth had to remind himself that in India extended families were still more or less the rule. But lack of privacy may not have been the problem. Siddharth showed the patient a stack of pictures: fashion models, female and male, nudes, ink blots he had brought from the United States. "Say the first thing that comes to your mind," Siddharth instructed.

The patient didn't say much. Siddharth asked about his friends and reminded him in Hindi that everything he said would be held in strict confidence.

Toward the end of his hour, the man began to speak about his friendship with a class-mate who had married a year before him, how they walked together for hours, even now, on the beach, where they stayed until long after dark. "He has a son," the patient said. "He shows me. With my wife, I cannot."

Siddharth leaned back in his chair. "Your problem is not what you can or cannot do. It is the fact that society has got you married and expects you to live as a heterosexual."

The man never made a second appointment. "What did you do to him?" Ashok asked. "He's in such a state! I have had to prescribe antidepressants."

"He doesn't need drugs," Siddharth said. "Send him back to me."

"You? You're the one who did this to him."

"No one makes a homosexual," Siddharth said.

"Homosexual? I send you a good Indian boy, perhaps a slight bit immature, and you show him dirty pictures? His whole family is upset about it!"

"I promised him the strictest confidentiality," Siddharth said.

"You had better give up dirty pictures, doctor, and buy a stethoscope," Ashok said.

Siddharth saw a few other referrals,

patients complaining about painful, sometimes debilitating ailments that his friends from med school couldn't cure. But his patients rarely made enough appointments to establish the necessary relationship, and he wasn't able to break even.

He bought an advertisement in one of the magazines that lay around the house. American psychoanalysts advertised, after all; he had seen their names in public-television magazines. But he could not bear the sight of his own name staring up at him like the man from Dostoyevsky's underground, superfluous, ridiculous. As Sid Doktor, M.D., Doctor of Psychiatry, he had been successful. Now, an idle buffoon from America who pored over outdated journals, he could not recognize himself.

He gave up the office and tried practicing at home, moving his desk into the darkened drawing room, closed off from the bedrooms by a door with velvet curtains on either side. Mina sent the servant in with tea. When no patients came, she brought in her tea and sat across the desk from him, her body plump and fluid in her silk sari. In San Jose, he had thought of her as fat.

"You could easily find a position in a hospital," she said.

"Mina, you don't know! Urine in the corridors, tormented souls —"

"It's only work," she said. "In the evenings you have your family."

"It is going backward, Mina. Those years in the hospital were preparation — "

"You are so American."

"I'm not," he said. "I'm caught between a lifestyle my whole family prefers and my career, where I can make enough money to support you."

"We cannot go back," said Mina, stiffening unnaturally in the chair. "Our sons are playing cricket."

"Cricket is not an Indian game!"

"It is more Indian than those boys who sit across your desk and complain about their families, their lovers, and their jobs."

"Homosexuals live everywhere."

"But we don't encourage such things. Do you want our sons to grow up where people think only of themselves? To do things that those patients of yours tell you about — "

"It's my job, Mina! If I stay in this country, what kind of future can we expect? My ability to bring in money is the only thing that stands between us and the beggars that follow my father home."

His mother called from the divan, where she was lying. "You must not trouble your wife with your work. The secret to a happy married life is to keep your secrets to yourself."

They told the children he was going back to San Jose only until Christmas, when he would always be able to come for two or three weeks.

"Why can't you stay here?" asked Sonny.

"Because I want to give you everything," he said.

"Can you bring us a pool?" Gautham asked.

But only Tara asked the question that Siddharth could not answer: "What about us? Are you just going to leave us here, as if we weren't born there?"

"It's not as if he's going there to settle," Mina said.

"You can come when school is out," Siddharth said, "in the summer."

"That doesn't get me out of this uniform," said Tara.

"You will be coming back for college," he said. "It's only a few years away." He knew, as his children couldn't, how quickly the time could pass.

He would see his wife when Christians sing the praises of their God; she would be in her natural element, from which her marriage, Siddharth realized, should never have uprooted her. She would bring the children to California every summer. What was so unusual, Siddharth wondered. People all over India left their families for months out of the year to make money they could not make in their villages. Mina would be faithful, he was sure, in the society of ladies' parties that she loved. As for himself, he did not know; he was a man.

He took a taxi alone to the airport. Mina, his mother, and his sister had obligations: if they did not go to their card party, they would each have to pay a fine for missing their contribution to the kitty. The boys had a cricket match. Siddharth hugged his daughter. "I don't want to leave you. Try to understand: my work, and your living."

"My living," Tara said. "Thanks a lot."

Siddharth touched Mrs. Singh's arm as he led her back toward his waiting room, where he could hear her daughter-in-law shouting at her children. "Go to India as soon as possible," he advised her. "Stay until you miss your children so much that your brothers and sisters cannot ease the pain."

He felt a tightness in his throat. It had been three months since he had been to India.

Mina and the kids would not be coming for another six weeks. He opened the polished oak door into the waiting room, smiled at the pale young man surrounded by Mrs. Singh's bored and tired grandchildren, and told him, "Give me just a minute. The receptionist will send you in."

➤ The Housewarming ➤

The thing is, Sally, you must bless everything big you receive — a new house, a husband, a male child. Fundamentally you have nothing against counting your blessings. Privately, like when you lay down to sleep. But you'd rather not have a public religious ceremony in your own house. You are just the wife, though — the girl, they called you at your wedding ten years ago. Your husband, Deshi, is the head of the family now, dutifully obeying his parents, who moved into your new house only one month after the closing. "Just humor them," he said when they first brought up this house blessing. "When you're their age, all you've got is festivals and family. Besides, if we don't do it, they'll nag us until we do. They'll never go back to India."

You give the priest two hundred dollars, and he promises to read the holy book start to finish, only getting up when an assistant or an interested Sikh relieves him. In an ideal world, you would volunteer your male relations, the way you tell your patients' family and friends to donate blood. But your father and brother wouldn't come to a religious service, and even your husband and his cousins can't read their mother tongue. Deshi's father reads until he breaks into a fit of coughing so bad that your mother-in-law has to run into the kitchen and tell the priest to put down his glass of Coke without ice and take back the pulpit.

They started reading Thursday in the *gurdwara*, a split-level converted into a temple by the local Sikh association. On Saturday morning, coincidentally Halloween, they drive the book twenty miles past the K-Mart to your house, where they set up a little sanctuary in your living room. You don't have to worry about moving furniture; you haven't had the time to buy any in the three months since you moved in. You did accompany your mother-in-law from store to store looking for a white sheet that was not fitted with elastic, edged with polyester lace, or dotted with little white-on-white fleurs-de-lis, designer signed. They've spread the sheet on the floor and taped a canopy to your ceiling. When you take it down, it will pull off four little one-inch squares of brand-new paint, but for now it looks exotic, like a golden tent in the desert.

Under the canopy they put the book — the size of a library dictionary — on a

pedestal a foot off the floor; they cover the bind-
ing with another cloth of gold. The priest sits
behind it, cross-legged, his white beard flowing
like a spray of Spanish moss. Next to him another old man in a white turban sits behind a
harmonium, an Indian accordion that stands on
the floor like a child's piano. With one hand he
plays, while with the other he opens and closes
a bellows in the back.

Beside him sits a third man, young, his
black beard long and lush, silently moving his
lips and staring at the sheet on the floor.

People come and go, their feet bare, their
heads covered with scarves, handkerchiefs,
veils, the ends of their saris, out of respect for the
book. Your husband's cousins are there. So is the
blonde in the family, Goodie, in from California
with her husband, her four small children, and
her mother-in-law, *your* mother-in-law's crazy
sister. You ask Goodie what possessed her to
drag the family such a distance. She glances
at her mother-in-law, raises her eyebrows, and
says, "She misses family." Deshi's cousin on his
father's side, Surinder, has divorced his American wife, Grace, and married a nineteen-year-
old from the Punjab, who is already pregnant.
The sweep of her black hair in your kitchen
threatens you, leaving you with only Goodie
as an ally in this great mistake you've come

135

to call your marriage. Goodie, who has such a strong Scandinavian identification that you're inclined to see her as a foreigner herself; Goodie, pregnant again, who already has enough kids to populate the entire family; Goodie, who has been raging ever since a pedophile cruising the mall praised her children for their big brown eyes, chocolate hair, and permanent tans: "Where did you ever get them?"

Goodie tells this story every time the family has a function, her pink face reddening as she builds up to the punch line: "My children don't even look like me; everybody thinks they're adopted!"

Hermeet and Surinder both wear turbans over their uncut hair. But every kid in the house has had a haircut. Even the pureblooded little Sikhs have escaped having their hair pulled into tight braids and pinned on top of their heads. You once asked their parents why. "In America they will be teased," the parents said. "Americans will call them hippie, Charles Manson, or the Fairy Queen."

You know the scene; you've seen it all before — at weddings, babies' namings, any excuse that the older generation can use to remember India. In fact, you've actually managed to miss half of this ceremony, having spent the morning with Nina, your husband's thirteen-year-old second cousin, buying trays of curried lentils and fried farmer's cheese floating in a sea of briny peas.

You locate Deshi, standing in the back yard with a glass of Scotch and some other forty-year-old boys. "I refuse to have any more to do with the food," you tell him, sniffing your hands to locate the exact source of the turmeric that you've been smelling all the way from Edison.

"Go make an appearance at the prayer," he says. "It's almost over. Please."

In your house the scent of incense has drowned out the smell of curry. You never can smell incense without remembering the taste of marijuana, and if you still smoked it, you wouldn't mind altering your consciousness with a joint right now. People you don't know, drinking Coke and orange juice in your kitchen, turn their eyes to your pumps clicking across the kitchen tiles. You saw their discarded wing tips, Reeboks, and Mary Janes in your garage.

You catch sight of your brother's daughter, yellow haired, like you when you were two. She runs across the kitchen and grabs the spangled scarf your mother-in-law gave you to wear on occasions like this. When you modeled the Punjabi suit your mother-in-law had made for you, your husband said, "I don't much like *chunis*." But you are like your brother's child:

anything pretty is worth wrapping around your head. Only after you'd been married six or seven years did you discover that the long, translucent scarves Indian women match so carefully with their clothes are not just for covering their heads in the presence of God, but for hiding their faces when an older man walks into the room.

You cast the *chuni* to your niece, and she squeals and covers her translucent face with it. Your sister-in-law came to this ceremony out of curiosity, perhaps, or maybe nostalgia for the exotic rituals she left behind with the sixties. You'd like to think she came with the intention of lending you a little moral support. "Your brother would never be able to take this," she mutters.

To pay your respects, you must retrieve the *chuni*. You know you must be seen bowing before the book once, or your mother-in-law will grumble. Besides, it's your house they're blessing.

You will have to lower your head to the floor in front of the book while one priest is reading, one is praying, and the third is singing. You must throw at least a dollar in front of the book, where a pile of paper money has already mounted up like the leaves waiting for collection in the gutter. When you used to go to church on Christmas and Easter, offerings were sealed in an envelope with a full-color picture of Jesus on it, so everyone would know you had put something in the basket but nobody would know how much.

While you're hesitating, Nina's mother pushes her into the room, head covered with a muffler pilfered from your closet. "Mom!" the teenybopper cries, and she runs out to the yard.

Your brother's child won't relinquish your *chuni*, so you pick her up, spread an end of it over both your heads, and carry her into the prayer room. She sits on your lap on the floor, next to a family friend who looks great in a street-length summer suit.

The harmonium wheezes shut and the priest starts talking. You think you recognize a few words — God, house, and Iqbal Singh, your father-in-law — but you have never been able to convince yourself, as soon as they start speaking Punjabi, that they're not talking about you, so you hug your niece, and she grips your bangles with her little pink fingers. Then she gets up and runs to the other room, where her mother has been watching from a safe distance.

The youngest priest, his beard flowing like the beard of Jesus, stands up and presses his palms together. Now you're going to have to pray. You think you recognize the word for wife, which he repeats over and over again, and you know he's talking about you; it's not just paranoia.

Back in the kitchen, Goodie is drinking beer and informing Surinder's new wife why Surinder divorced Grace. Her youngest slides a glass off the counter. "Oh, bad, Hergobinder." Goodie sighs, and he breaks into a wail. She comforts him while you rush in to pick up the larger pieces, dodging his brothers and sisters, who have filled your kitchen. You mutter to Nina, "Take them trick-or-treating."

"We're not wearing costumes," she says.

Hergobinder is wearing a pair of white leggings, tight on his doll-like calves, and a miniature Nehru jacket. Nina is wearing a pair of skin-tight orange and blue Day-Glo pants and a long T-shirt with Mickey Mouse on the front, his ears hanging from her breasts, which are already larger than yours, "Mickey died for our sins" inscribed across her belly.

"Take them out to the yard," you say.

"I was supposed to go to a party," she whines.

The doorbell rings. Your father-in-law opens the door to a man his age, in khakis and a shirt, and a four-year-old, her fair hair teased into a pony tail, her short legs showing beneath a pink tutu. You drop a Milky Way into her plastic pumpkin. In the room adjoining the hall, the priest is still droning on. You long to go trick-or-treating with this couple, the way you used to, perfectly costumed and disguised. "What are you?" you ask.

"Can't you guess?" the little girl says. "Jeez, where have you been?"

"Madonna," her grandfather says. He watches your father-in-law shuffle back into the living room.

"House-blessing prayer," you tell him.

The little girl says, "What does that old man keep under his big hat?"

"Hair."

"He looks like Santa Claus."

You think about that: white beard, belly, red silk shirt.

"It's not Christmas," she says. You nod. "It's Halloween." Your favorite holiday. "It's a good costume anyway."

You drag out the vacuum and go after Hergobinder's glass, drowning out the rest of the young priest's syllables — *wife, children, God*. When he stops, Deshi rushes into the kitchen and says, "Serve! The priests are going to another party."

Later Deshi and his father drive the priests to their second party, leaving you to bid the guests good-bye. They pat your shoulder, tell you that you must come to Hoboken, Jersey

City, Jackson Heights. You make a lot of promises you'll never keep. The sun goes down. A
band of kids dressed up as bums, monsters, skel-
etons, and superheroes stares at these depart-
ing men and women in turbans, pajamas, leisure
suits, and saris; they turn back toward the road,
as if they think your house might be the kind
that gives out razor blades.

Goodie and her brood crowd into your
kitchen while you wash the dishes. "Another
splendid family reunion," she says.

Your brother's wife has gone, taking your
niece with her. You wanted to go too, back to
Cherry Hill, where your psychedelic friends used
to talk about Eastern religions as if they knew
what they were talking about. You wonder if
Goodie has ever shared your fantasy of escaping
from the family, but you never ask. Rumor has
it Goodie has "walked around somebody else's
holy book" before.

When Deshi comes back, all his cousins
are gone but Hermeet and family, who will be
crashing in your new guest rooms. You tell your
father-in-law that he might as well go to bed like
your mother-in-law and Hermeet's mother, but
he wants to sit around in the prayer room a little
longer, even though it has been stripped down
to an empty living room again.

It's early, but you rush upstairs. You leave

your Punjabi suit on the floor and crawl between the sheets. Your husband comes in. "Did you meet the priest?"

"I couldn't exactly miss him."

"First thing he said when we got into the car: 'You didn't introduce me to your wife.' "

"Not 'Which one was your wife?' What did he say, the young one — when the music stopped and he got started?"

Deshi laughs and puts his arms around you. He smells like incense, Scotch. "Something like: 'It is the duty of the mother to teach the children the religion.' "

"What children? What religion?"

Deshi turns out the light. A harvest moon shines through the few remaining leaves of the oak outside your window. You hope that all the trick-or-treaters have gone home. Soon even your father-in-law will stop praying and go to bed, and some forgotten Celtic lord will call forth the dead. And you without so much as a jack-o'-lantern to scare them away. Deshi tightens his arms around you. You will never know in this life whether you've been tricked or treated, cursed or blessed.

⇝ Home Is Where ⇜ the Heart Grows Fonder

Darji lay in bed in the middle of the eight-room house surrounded by jungle. At least in India that is what he would have called Stirling, New Jersey, where Surinder, his son, had bought his second house. He was listening to the priest singing his niece's marriage ceremony, which he had recorded almost twenty years ago. The sweet wheezing of the harmonium, the beat of the *tabla* played out on the cassette unaccompanied by any traffic on the road, which was, at any rate, more than a hundred yards from his window. His son had told him in the morning: *Sorry. I have to go . . . business . . . two days.* His daughter-in-law had gone back to India with his granddaughter. She was the second wife of Darji's only son, whom the family had found for Surinder after his marriage to the American, Grace, had ended in divorce. Whether this wife would come back to America or not, Darji couldn't say. It was her duty to take care of her husband's parents, but instead she was living in her own parents' house. She had a duty to her child, she said.

Darji's wife had also gone home to India, but only to take care of her sister, who had had a heart attack. Darji knew all about heart attacks. He'd had his first in India, not long after Surinder's second marriage. Darji's daughter had insisted that he go back to America to live with Surinder, though he had not wanted to worry his son. Surinder was no longer the carefree boy that he had been in India. Darji's daughter had tried to live in America too, but she'd gone back, too old now to marry. Darji had not done his duty by her.

The doctors said that he could not survive another heart attack, which they could not prevent. So much pain. American machines had kept his heart from failing. Surgeons had operated. He had gone home to Surinder's first house in the south of Jersey. He might live for five, ten years, the doctors promised him.

Once a husband and a father, a father-in-law twice, a grandfather, now wherever he might lie, he was alone. Who would rush him to a hospital if the heartburn that had started after he had heated up the Chinese food turned out to be angina? Surinder had shown him the button on the telephone, sitting on the table by his bed, but he could not see. American medicine had saved his life, but it could not restore his sight. Old age, the doctor had told him, a consequence of living longer than the veins behind his eyes. If he should shout in the night, not even a neighbor lived close enough to come to his aid. In India at least the house servant would run to him, his bare feet slapping on the floor while the neighborhood night watchmen and pariah dogs called to each other in the streets.

His son would come the next evening, he knew, pour himself a glass of Scotch and ice, and carry his briefcase past the bedroom, where he might look in and find his father, fallen to the carpet between the beds. No breath, no pain. Surinder drops his drink, falls to his knees, shouts, but no one but Surinder hears. In touching his father's cold, stiff body, Surinder cannot bear to straighten out the leg twisted at an angle that Darji would never have been able to achieve in life, even when he was a young man with a beautiful wife, a pretty daughter, and a beloved, long-awaited son.

❯❯ A White Woman's ❮❮ Burden

I'm sitting with my husband's sister, following the sun across the courtyard of her New Delhi house. Hawkers shout beyond the wall between the courtyard and the alley: *"Gajar!"* "Carrots," I say. *"Pyaza!"* My nephew passes through, taller than his father, and casts a smile that would attract women in any culture.

"In one year he will go to college in America," Sita says. She sighs. "It took me seven years to get this son."

Two possibilities: she's trying to console me for fourteen years of childless marriage; she's trying to find out what has prevented me from getting pregnant.

"I never wanted children," she says. "I was afraid of that kind of pain."

Three trips to India and my husband's parents in my house in New Jersey should have accustomed me to the contradictions of my husband's family, but Sita has surprised me. Not four years married and she had a daughter. Then she bore this son.

"I had trouble," she says, "from the time I started taking the medicine."

"The pill?"

"Pills were supposed to make me fertile. They only made me sick."

"Fertility pills? What changed your mind?"

"My mother-in-law was keen on a grandson."

So is mine, but she has not convinced me to take on major physical change, more responsibility, another human being to invade my privacy for eighteen years.

"We went on pilgrimage," Sita says. "Nothing worked. After Susheela was born we took a trip to Goa. Just for holiday. There are temples in Goa. And there is a church. One of your saints is on display."

"Francis," I say, not that any saint could be considered mine.

"You must go to Goa."

We're planning on it. Despite my fear of flying, which has been growing since the Iranian hostage crisis, Deshi and I try to take a winter vacation every year — Jamaica, Cancun, the U.S. Virgin Islands. I can't let our first trip to India in nine years deprive me of a beach.

"You must see the remains of this saint," Sita goes on. "You just write your request on a chit. A priest will read it and pray to the saint."

"I'm not Catholic," I say.

"It does not matter. You could be Sikh like me."

"I thought you'd converted to Hinduism."

"We are Hindu. Even Ram said, 'Why not?' And I wrote down my request for a son. When I came back, I conceived. I've got a lot of faith after that."

"In Christianity?"

"In general."

I envy her. I have little faith that I will even make it back to Short Hills. Two days before we left JFK, a bomb blew the cockpit off a 747 — same airline as ours, same return flight — and 259 people went down across a thirty-mile stretch of Scotland. Deshi tried to calm me by saying that the probability of a bomb on two flights in the same week was the same as the chance of a meteor's hitting the plane. But Deshi's logic has never been able to console me. I don't listen to him anymore. I married him to be alone with him, but I could never count on six months going by without someone from his family moving in. I have no faith in the future I planned.

I have patients with irrational fears of

illnesses or certain spaces, but in 1989, a fear of violence, of being killed by a bomb in an airplane, seems to me legitimate. Still, thirty-nine years of television and middle-class prejudice had me imagining a flame-thrower in the hands of the tall, black American who stood in the back of the plane. "This is a long flight," he said, when he caught me looking at him. Suspicion turned to shame. Then in Frankfurt, where Pan Am 103 had taken off, I stood helplessly by while a security guard took Deshi into an office for questioning. My husband is dark enough to make whites suspicious, but he is just as Aryan as I, by language group if not by race; our ancestors just happened to migrate in opposite directions. In the end I obeyed a shouting, fair-haired German in uniform and boarded the plane. When we taxied past El Al, guards with their Uzis on the roof, I almost wished we were leaving Germany with a country in an active state of war.

In the land of Gandhi, terrorism is no more under control. When we go out with Deshi's youngest sister's husband, who wears a turban, the police stop us to search the car. Delhi maintains a state of alert — police checks at the crossroads, the street to the prime minister's house blocked. The day we fly to Goa, January 6, 1989, the government hangs two Sikhs for the assassination of Indira Gandhi. Our plane is held up all afternoon. Even for a domestic flight we're both frisked, on the chance that a Sikh terrorist might use our plane to avenge the executed zealots. Deshi's in a delicate position: to a Hindu, his name is Sikh; to a Sikh terrorist, his haircut is an act of treason.

By the time we reach the beach, the sun has set. A policeman, his rifle cradled in his arms, watches as we immerse ourselves in the Arabian Sea. "Why do they need a guard?" I ask. "Terrorism this far from Delhi?"

"Hippies," Deshi says.

"So this is where the flower children looked for God," though I suspect the English and American youths who meditated on this beach were more interested in a tan than transcendence. Goa is beautiful enough, though, to attract a god, the sand ivory in the dark, the salt water as warm as a bath, amniotic. Our slowing pulses synchronize with the waves, and I take comfort in the mother from which we all have come. But as soon as I turn back toward the hotel, I see the guard with his automatic rifle.

We spend mornings in the sea, afternoons in bed. My brother-in-law's unheated house in Delhi was so cold that we had refused to move from beneath a pile of heavy quilts. Brown men serve us breakfast, clip the hedges

into the shapes of Goan fishing boats, and protect us from white hippie panhandlers. Most of
the other tourists in Majorda Beach are German, flown in direct from Frankfurt. Third-
world luxury is cheap for old- and new-world
travelers. There is not a child in the hotel. I
point this out to Deshi, and he reminds me how
few Indians can afford Goa, how Westerners
rarely bring their children on third-world winter
vacations.

On our last day in the sun, I look through
the *Goan English Daily* for news of riots, hi-
jackings, or assassinations that might compli-
cate our trip. I can't even find an article about
reactions to the executions, though the language dispute between the states of Karnataka
and Maharashtra has turned violent. On the last
page of the tabloid, I see a headline: "Spiritual
Enlightenment Supersedes Pleasure." Transcendence of the flesh, in my day, was what
India was all about. But everytime I've come,
I've only eaten well, bought block-printed silks
and tie-dyed cottons, and basked in the sun that
would not warm me for another four months.
According to the editorial, to achieve the
Hindu form of grace, a man must renounce
pleasure: "The purpose of life is to avoid rebirths." I can understand renunciation: I gave up
sleep for years to become a doctor. "To avoid

rebirths" is more problematic. Though reincarnation does not seem possible, anything that might offer a second chance has always appealed to me. But Hindus believe that life is hell, the liberation from this life the only heaven worth living for. Every time I see a leper tapping on the taxi window with his stump, I must agree: life *is* hell. But I have no compensating faith in heaven.

I remember how I once felt the presence of the Hindu goddess Ganga in a temple high above the Ganges, and I think that if I could share Sita's willingness to believe, I might be able to control my fear. So I ask Deshi to forgo one last day on the beach to visit the churches his sister told me about. We hire a taxi and ride through palm groves and cashew orchards lining the country roads. Brick and stucco sanctuaries dot the road — inside each a cross and technicolor Jesus lit with candles and garlanded with marigolds, just like the Hindu gods we've seen in peoples' *puja* corners. Goans trudge along the dusty roads, their mustaches black against their swarthy faces. In Old Goa we pass more Germans, their legs bare and burnt by an unfamiliar sun. The street widens. Privet hedges trimmed immaculately in the European style lead us to the churches, stone and stucco, their baroque steeples exotic in a land of turrets, minarets, and domes. Hawkers peddle ice cream, balloons, and jaundiced candles, the kind Sita has pledged to light for Chotu. Deshi and I go inside. The Bom Jesus Basilica seems curiously bare — no pews on the uneven cobbled floor, no stations of the cross below the dull, tinted windows high up in the wooden walls, no frescoes on the vaulted ceiling. The statue of some saint stares down, flanked by the mother and child, dressed up and white faced, as the Hindus represent their gods. A few Goans wander in. A Punjabi couple, pale by South Indian standards, gazes into an alcove on the side of the altar, the new wife's hands and feet still reddened with elaborate paisleys and flowers. She wants a son; perhaps she's come to request one.

Deshi dips his hand into the holy water and makes the sign of the cross. He sprinkles me, the way he does when we visit a *gurdwara*, but I don't feel blessed, not even comforted, let alone spiritually enlightened. A guide points out the body of St. Francis, high on a platform twenty feet above the floor. Behind the glass of the casket I think I see a skull cap and hands pressed into a prayer.

"That's the actual body?" Deshi asks. "I can't see anything."

"Security is necessary," the guide says.

"One lady bit off a toe. It bled, just as if the saint were still alive."

"They must have embalmed him," Deshi says.

"They did nothing," the guide says. "It is a miracle."

I'm as skeptical as my husband. Nor does the preservation of even a good missionary's body strike me as a worthwhile way for God to spend His time. Why can't God with one stroke make the hearts of the rich and powerful more generous?

Against the wall beside me is a box labeled "Requests for the Saint," a pen, and slips of paper like the one on which Sita must have written her request for a son. What do I want? Life. But I'm referring to my own. It takes faith to bear a child. I can't feel that faith, not yet, not even in the church where Sita thinks she got her son. "Give," I tell the saint. *Datta.* In Delhi a man called out — "Sahib!" — so twisted that he had to walk on his hands and feet, his back permanently parallel to the ground. When Deshi gave him a rupee, he held it to his forehead, kissed it, pressed it to his chest. My heart went out to him: *Dayadvam.*

Damyata, as if I were in control of my life.

Outside again, I see the candles burning in an iron grate, pallid in the blinding sun. I could have bought one, touched it to a flame that someone else had lit, and fixed it in the lattice with the others. But I'm afraid I will not feel Sita's rush of faith. I am sure no saint can give me a child.

From the church we ride directly to the airport. All the flights are late. We sit on the floor and watch the German tourists smoothing their souvenir pajamas over their bellies. They can be complacent; I've never heard of a Lufthansa going down. A tall Sikh, rare in Goa, walks past, and I wonder what he's carrying in his metal briefcase. I hope he isn't on our flight. I lean against my husband. "I'm afraid to fly," I say.

He shakes me off. In India men and women don't touch in public. "Don't be stupid," he says.

"I'm afraid of the future," I say.

"No, you're not."

I want to tell him I'm afraid of having children too, but I sense he's heard enough. I stand up and pace the airport lounge, women all around me darting after toddlers before they can dash into the automatic rifles of the police.

"Do you want a sandwich?" Deshi asks.

"I'm too nervous to eat."

He walks off to buy one anyway.

By the time we board, another sunny day has come and gone. A frisker stands on the tarmac, rubbing down the men with a metal detector. When a woman stops, he waves her into the plane, his palm open and his head swinging laterally. As if Pan Am's bomb had not been carried by a woman.

My heart holds to the earth as the plane rises into a cloudless sky. I can't read. I can't eat the kebabs Deshi insists I try. I watch the sapphire coast of Malabar give way to the miles and miles of sandstone that gave this land its holy saffron color. Every now and then the one-lane roads and mud huts of a village break the monotony. Emerald green hill stations dot the countryside, a crystal lake. While I am watching India slip by, I am not conscious of my racing heart, the tiny silver beads of sweat I've left on the metal armrest.

Back in Delhi, I suggest we hire a car and spend our last two days in Rajasthan, where sandstone forts tried for centuries to hold back the future. To ride up a steep hill to the Amber Palace, Deshi persuades me to sit with him on the back of an elephant. It sways leisurely, its tough hide painted like the hands of an Indian bride, as we approach the walls of the abandoned palace. I do not look down. Women who once lived inside these golden walls burned themselves to death to escape the hands of their husbands' enemies. I can almost feel them trying to protect their sons from the battles they must risk their lives in, their daughters from the pains of childbirth. They are here. All of them. Just beyond the crumbling walls. In the secluded courtyards, behind marble screens, in the very air of India itself.

They try to tell me that anything is possible: hope, faith, love, a life that will not end in being hurled out of the sky.

Two weeks later I will test my urine to confirm what I have diagnosed while Deshi and I sat on the long return flight, so uneventful that I won't even remember it. I'll continue to struggle between uncanny pride and the fear that I will never be able to dispel in a terrifying world. I'm thirty-nine. I don't need an obstetrician to tell me that I've waited long enough to incur risks. When I take this child to India, I'll be frightened by the new responsibility I've taken on. But I will have to find the faith. At least I'll have to fake it.

America the Beautiful

Three years after I was deported from the USA, I sit in the middle of a double bed in New Delhi, wrapped up in the reds and golds of a typical Indian bride. My second cousin, Susheela, who was matched up, married, and knocked up so fast that I hardly recognize her, sits in front of me painting little flowers on my hands. "Nina," she says, "Did you hear?"

"I don't understand Punjabi."

"How is it that you do not understand Punjabi?" asks her mother, squeezed onto the bed beside her. "Your own mother tongue!"

"My own mother never speaks it. Except when one of you is visiting."

As usual no one listens. Susheela's grandmother, in for the occasion from New Jersey, hobbles in and mutters something else I can't understand. She raised my mother when my grandmother died, so I guess she's like a grandmother to me, though my mother's always had mixed feelings. I can hear the men of the family laughing in the courtyard. Aunt Sita, the grandmother-to-be, says in English for my benefit, "Our cousin-sister should be here."

"My mother can't be here," I say. "American immigration would never let her back."

This aunt, cousin, whatever, has the nerve. She didn't even have to live in America to get her green card. Uncle Ram's brother sponsored Ram's whole family. But Uncle Ram will never leave India — unless an emergency like war, disease, or bankruptcy forces him out. He got the family green cards so that Chotu, his son, would be able to work legally in the United States.

I was born in this community of overdressed women and spoiled men. But my mother got us out, and we lived with one cousin after another across the Middle East, Africa, and England, chasing the setting sun of the British Empire. When I was six, we moved to New Jersey. My mother had first and second cousins, Deshi and Hermeet, who wrote letters to the U.S. embassy in London promising to put us up, so we could get tourist visas. We overstayed our visas for thirteen years. It was possible back then for a tourist in the United States to get a Social Security card, so my mother flipped hamburgers at Burger King even though it wasn't legal.

But by the time I turned sixteen, immigration law in the U.S. had gotten more restrictive. Only legal residents could get Social Security cards, and without a Social Security number, I couldn't work, couldn't get a driver's license, couldn't apply for scholarships unless I could show a foreign student visa.

My mother tried to get us legal residency, paying lawyers, mostly, who all said that without a sponsor, permanent residence would be virtually impossible. And cousins cannot sponsor each other. She tried to argue that her closest relative in the United States was not merely a cousin but a cousin-brother. In India, cousins are raised as brothers and sisters. Mom's first cousins were expected to take care of her, like brothers.

I used to think that if only I knew my cousins, I would feel like I belonged somewhere. Then one by one they started coming over. Sonya from South Africa had been my idol. A graduate student at the University of California, she wore jeans with large, exotic shirts, so that everyone would know that she was just like them but somehow foreign. Surinder Kaur came from Delhi a few years later. She was even richer than Sonya, but since India restricts the amount of money travelers can take out, she was always broke. Chotu was the third to come, when his father had to be in the United States for his interview with the Immigration and Naturalization Service.

It must have had something to do with the way I had always felt in America, not white and not black either, most comfortable with friends whose grandparents did not speak English, whether they had come from Italy, Puerto Rico, or China. I had the feeling I'd known Chotu all my life. He was genuinely, certifiably hot. Here's what I didn't know, or didn't understand, at the time: he loved girls — women; he was used to getting what he wanted; he did not believe he could be wrong. Put them all together. He stayed with us a week before his parents took him up to Yale. We spent every night talking. Then we ran out of things to say and made love. I was careful. The last thing I needed was to finish school in a maternity ward.

He knew all about my visa problem. "If there's anything I can do," he said, "just ask. You're my cousin, little cousin. The future of the family is in America. Even my sister would come if my dad would let her out of his sight before he gets her married."

"You can't marry your cousin."

"Muslims marry their cousins. Even Parsis."

"So what are you saying?"

"Why doesn't your mother get married? To an American, I mean. Old Americans are always getting married."

I didn't want to share our apartment with a man. I had never wanted to share my mother with anybody. But I used to wonder why Mom didn't date. Something about Indians not remarrying, how unhappy she had been. I often wondered if my father were still alive. Mom tried to be honest: "I don't know, Nina. After you and I left, someone told me that he died in an earthquake. Or he was murdered by a terrorist. Why should I struggle to find a man who beat me, who thought girls were not worth having?"

Then she would break down, as she always did. "Damn my damned cursed luck."

Something I inherited from her. If I'd been able to get a driver's license, I'd have driven up to New Haven to see Chotu every weekend — if I'd had a car — but whenever I suggested he come down, he said he had a lot to do, he would come as soon as he had a little break. I was so happy just to talk to him that it never occurred to me that I was always the one who called.

I graduated first in my class from Parsippany Hills High School. It seemed the least I could do, since I couldn't bring home any

163

money, couldn't solve our immigration problems, couldn't even spend my weekends with Chotu. With my mother's Social Security number and help from Deshi, I got into a university that did not ask to see a green card, one in a warmer climate. That was when my mother really lost it: "My life is over. My only child is gone. Without daughter, how will mother live? Who will be here when I come home from work? Why should I work? My life is over."

"It's not as if you're going to die without me," I said, guilty as a felon. "I'll be back for Thanksgiving, Christmas, spring break, and all summer long, since I can't just go out and get a job in Louisiana."

"You cannot go out and get a job," she said. "I got a job, and look at me: no specialty to make me eligible for the green card. You must be a doctor, engineer, or these computers. Then a company will sponsor you. Then you can sponsor me."

I could never figure my mother out. On the one hand, she was brave enough to risk deportation. On the other, she was so afraid of being sent back to India that she never stopped worrying about it. She'd come home and have a Scotch to cut the pain in her legs. Soon she was crying: "Five years with my cousin-sisters in those crazy places! In Africa they hate us because Indians are rich and neither white or black. Even England called us blackies. I thought in America I could belong!"

I never had to ask her why she'd left. She never stopped talking about the cows, flies, beggars, and women like her, dependent for their survival on their husbands. And she was right. Just outside Aunt Sita's house, as I sit here on her bed, women stand wrapped in rags, naked babies in their arms. They know from the tent blocking the street that a wedding will be taking place, that there will be food, and money from the hands of guests guilty about their luck.

I never made it through my first semester of college. I wanted Chotu so much more than a degree. "Please, please, please," I said. "This is the state of Jerry Lee Lewis. He married *his* cousin."

"It couldn't be forever," Chotu said.

"Nothing lasts forever."

"Stop crying," he said. "I'll come down for fall break. It's too cold up here already."

He was coming. He was finally coming. But for just one week? "You have to stay. Immigration will find out. They'll think we're faking it because we live in different states."

"We don't have to give them different addresses. Besides, who says married couples have to live together? One of my professors lives clear across the country from her husband. Immigration is too busy rooting out Arabs and Mexicans to care if a couple of A students want an open marriage. When your papers come through, we'll get divorced. It's easy. People do it all the time."

By marrying Chotu and getting my green card, I would be a legal American girl. I'd become a citizen and sponsor my mother. She already read *The Star Ledger* every day. She knew more about elections than I had learned in four years of social studies.

I begged my roommate to sleep in someone else's room. Lying in my bunk with Chotu was all I had wanted for so long that I almost forgot to buy a license. We filed my papers the same day that the judge signed our marriage certificate. Then Chotu flew back to Connecticut.

I have no idea why Immigration and Naturalization investigated our marriage. An agent must have noticed that the address we'd given was a college dormitory for unmarried students. I received an order to depart within ten days.

I was afraid they might arrest me, put me in jail. Or, worse, trace me to my mother and deport her for something I had done. So I called her from the airport. "Don't follow me to India," I said. "You'll never make it back."

"Why should I come back?" she said. "My life is over."

"Let's just call this trip a visit," I said. "Don't go anywhere. I'm coming back. As soon as I can get a student visa."

"Why did you do it? You were going to college. You would get a job."

"That would take too long."

"For what?"

"Mom, I couldn't stand waiting! Neither could you! I was just trying to make things a little easier!"

The flight to India was long. I could hardly stand up by the time I made it through the long line for "natives," trying to explain to jabbering officials that I didn't speak Hindi. My mother must have called. The entire family was at the airport — Susheela, Aunt Sita, her eyes red, even Uncle Ram, his face a stern mask.

I spent weeks in bed while the family peeked in, at first only asking why I slept so much, then pushing me out of bed. Uncle Ram took me to the embassy. Indian clerks promised to consider my application for a student visa, but they needed this paper and that. When I called my mother, all she could do was cry. Chotu took on the tone of his father: "Nina, what's going on? My mother says you won't get out of bed. If you can't get a visa, go to college there. You can come back here for grad school."

"That's years away. And who's to say I'll get in, get a visa? You're my cousin, my brother, my husband —"

That was as far as I ever got before my aunt snatched away the receiver and piled the Punjabi on him.

Then there was the matter of my record. If you lie on an application, you might not be eligible for reentry. I told an Indian at the American embassy that I didn't lie; I was legally married.

My mother's cousins went out of their way never to mention the marriage. I slept, dreaming of Chotu. Every day I expected him, but he didn't turn up, not even for his summer vacation. I spent the hottest summer of my life without even a public pool. Then it rained. Susheela took me to her college. To give Uncle Ram credit, he got me in. But I couldn't understand the lectures. My professors had their Ph.D.'s from Princeton, Cornell, the Universities of Texas, California, Michigan. But that didn't make it any easier for me to understand their Indian English. And they didn't like me any better than my fellow students, who called me the American and, after a flurry of attention, avoided me. I missed American history, political science, American literature. Uncle Ram had enrolled me in calculus, economics, computer science. I was flunking for the first time in my life. Ram kept me in. Susheela taught me how to cheat. While I was struggling through my first year for the second time, she dropped out. We spent my second Indian summer in the mountains, so cool and green that I woke up crying every night. Chotu did not show. It was time to apply himself to making his career in the United States, his mother said. I hadn't spoken to him for a year.

In the fall, while I continued to be baffled by numbers, which Uncle Ram insisted were a universal language, Susheela looked through pictures, collected saris and Punjabi suits, sat for tea and cashews, and finally agreed to marry the boy her parents liked. Chotu topped that with an aerogram telling his mother that he had become engaged. His mother ran into the house in tears waving the flimsy blue paper. Shouts turned into whispers. "Who is she?" I asked. "How did he meet her?"

What did it matter? Someone must have signed annulment papers for me. The family denied that my marriage had taken place. I was even beginning to forget it myself, lying in bed all day, my head bursting with incomprehensible equations.

Chotu did not come for his own sister's wedding. He was in the middle of exams, Aunt Sita told the guests. He never came to get married himself, either. I didn't care. I was through with him. Through with men. Like my mother.

Then my mother's cousins started whispering in Sita's room, smiling as I passed, urging me not to study but to get some rest, I would ruin my eyes. After I had blown another set of exams — how do you write an essay in a math course? — Uncle Ram told me that it didn't make much sense to continue at the university when I could not distinguish myself in the major he had chosen. I was about to say that it might not be me that was flunking so much as the subjects he had enrolled me in, when Aunt Sita came in and told me, "We have found a way to get you back to America."

Chotu's first cousin on his father's side. Chotu had described him for me — long, straight hair, stripped of its natural black to a neon orange, face and body two shades blacker than his butt, earring in which ear Chotu could not remember, permanent marijuana haze.

"He is perfect for you," Aunt Sita said. "He has not finished a degree either. And the family is good — my husband's sister, who is settled in California. The boy is working at a shop.

He has prospects for the future. He is not a bad looking boy —"

"Does he have a green card?" I asked.

"He is an American citizen," she said. "He was born in California. My sister-in-law went to visit her brother and had the baby there."

I wanted to see this guy's passport before I would consent to marry him. Aunt Sita told me he would bring it. I knew I would be pushing my luck, but I asked: "Were there any other prospects?"

I stopped her before she could tell me it was hard to match a depressive, darker-than-most-of-the-family, deported, poor flunk-out who might not make it through her immigration interview and onto the plane, but who was desperate enough to be grateful to a middle-class family in California for taking her in, so desperate as to be in their debt forever, so slow that she could not possibly mind a dull, simple boy like Harry Paul Singh Rani.

Look out, Harry, I thought. I made up my mind that sleeping with him could not be any worse than not sleeping with anybody. I wouldn't have to sleep with him even on our wedding night if I could come up with a good excuse. The wedding had been planned around my cycles, but girls had been known to be irregular, especially girls who lie about in bed all day. At any rate, I would not be able to return to California with him. The wait for spouses had grown to almost two years as quotas shrank and the number of Indians wanting to immigrate increased. But I was used to waiting.

The designs on my hands are dry, and I get up to take off the old sari. My mother's sobs are still pulsing in my ears: "Nina, you do not have to marry any boy. I will marry. As soon as I can find some way to protect our money —"

"He's all right," I said.

"Are you sure?"

I had seen Harry only once. He sat in Aunt Sita's drawing room, his gaze bouncing off the filigree-papered walls, freaked on the country of his DNA, as I had been — either that, or from a stronger brand of *bhang* than he was used to. His mother, a doughy, simpering woman, praised me for not saying a word while they discussed my attributes; his father harumphed and bragged about Harry's prospects as manager-in-training of a surf and ski shop in Covina.

Even when they left us alone in the drawing room, a bold move with a doper and a divorcée, he said nothing about our impending marriage. Only, "Shit, it's hotter here than in the Valley."

This time I will immigrate to a warm suburb. I will ace the citizenship exam: George Washington, the Civil War, Alaska and Hawaii. A passport they can't take away. Then I will divorce the Surfer Dude and enroll in a program for adults returning to college. In-state tuition. I will sell the gold that my mother's cousins have been draping around my neck, arms, and head since I agreed to marry Harry. Maybe I will have to get my passport under Harry's name, maybe I will even have to sleep with him, but I will get that passport. Then I can sponsor my mother.

❧ Missing Persons ❧

Leslie had never been in love. She had gone to all the proms, some of the dances, a few fraternity parties, dinners and shows. She had even gone to bed. But the experience had never been as pleasurable as she had expected, and she had never wanted anyone enough to marry him. In her thirties she looked better than ever. Her skin had not aged, and her hair was in the process of frosting itself. She kept in shape; as an engineer with a multinational corporation, she could afford well-fitting, stylish suits and dresses. But as she progressed from technical staff to department head, her social life continued to decline. Everyone was just too busy. The pool of unmarried men diminished. She felt less and less sure that she would ever feel enough passion to exchange her one-bedroom condominium for a one-family house. When at thirty-five she began to despair of ever having children, she was sorry she had not searched as hard for a prospective husband and father as for a career. She was seriously contemplating calling a dating service when Surinder asked her out.

Surinder Singh had come to Bell Laboratories after RCA had laid him off. He'd met Leslie while he was still married to his second wife. After his wife and their daughter had gone back to India, he was spending twelve, thirteen hours a day at the labs, with the other single engineers. He would lean in the doorway of Leslie's office and talk: his wife was not coming back; he had so much wanted a son, but his wife had not been able to have another child; he was middle-aged; he had just turned forty. He had wasted so much time in America, almost twenty years. He didn't tell Leslie that she looked a bit too old to start a family. But he hadn't managed to seduce anybody younger with the aphrodisiacs in restaurant curries, the endorphins in the chilies, which, he told her, created a kind of orgasm of the palate.

Leslie grew accustomed to seeing Surinder's shoes by her condo door, the sweet, burning smell of curry on the stove, the hair that fell to his shoulders when he combed it out. She was attracted to the difference in him, but she never felt her heart stop when he came into her office. And she didn't think that she would miss him if she couldn't see him every day. But she went to bed with him, and when she found out she was pregnant she was overjoyed.

* * *

But the tall dark stranger is so familiar from romance novels that Surinder threatens the originality of this story. If authorial intervention made him a woman, she might take the plot in a different direction. Surinder's surname, Singh, identifies him as male; the surname Kaur is given to Sikh girls. A change of name and gender will begin another story.

Surinder Kaur won't meet her family's expectations: to become a doctor in the United States — her Uncle Deshi's wife, an American M.D., will get her into medical school; to marry, between the ages of twenty-one and twenty-five, a Punjabi Sikh settled in America, and to sponsor her father and mother for permanent residence, so that when her father sells the business, the family can be together again. By her second semester she's majoring in marketing and dating an American. Leslie Powers III is anything but what Surinder has been used to. A shock of yellow hair flips over his forehead, threatening to cascade into his pure, blue eyes. She doesn't sleep with him until she's sure she loves him, in the first warm days of spring, just before she flies to India for her summer vacation. In Delhi she longs for him, knowing, like the heroines of every movie she has ever seen, that any relationship as intense as this one must end in marriage.

Leslie suffers too. He has never known a girl so beautiful, so different from South Bend girls. He begs his father for a trip to India, to celebrate his acceptance into medical school, and before the end of summer, he is in New Delhi by Surinder's side.

Surinder's parents are not nearly as resistant as she has expected. They would have liked her to finish her degree before getting married. But Leslie is enrolled in medical school. At least one of them will be a doctor. And how can they send her back unmarried, since the entire neighborhood has seen the boy going in and out of their house?

So Surinder Kaur and Leslie Powers III fly back to Indiana married. Surinder starts her sophomore year. But in India putting off having a family is not in fashion. Get it over with, and a girl will still be young enough to wear her saris to her children's weddings. Surinder almost makes it through her second semester before she discovers she is pregnant.

In Surinder's family, it has always been traditional for a daughter to give birth in her parents' house, but Leslie Powers III will not hear of his wife's having a baby in India. Surinder has no choice but to ask her mother to come help her.

Since Leslie knows the nurses, they are more than happy to welcome his mother-in-law into the delivery room. But Mrs. Kaur's support breaks down, in Leslie's professional opinion, when she insists that he call the anesthesiologist: "For God's sake. Even in India we do not make a poor girl suffer."

Leslie tries to explain, "It's better for the baby if she does it without drugs. She's been through Lamaze. She can take it."

Surinder howls from the depths of her body.

"You heartless, white-haired bastard!"

Leslie and Mrs. Kaur never get along. Whenever he picks up the baby, she is there. If he pulls a blanket off because the child is sweating, she is at his elbow warning him not to let the baby catch a chill.

"They get fevers from overheating," Leslie says. "I'm in medical school, after all!"

"And a mother's natural instincts for her child are not to be trusted?"

Classes and exams keep Leslie out so late that he hardly sees his family. He comes home to discover Surinder and the baby sleeping together in his bed, and his heart catches. He tries to convince Surinder that it isn't safe to share the same bed with the baby. She could easily roll over and crush him. "Don't be ridiculous," she says. "I'd never roll over on my own son." She plays with the buttons on Leslie's shirt, her hair cascading down her back, her breasts, which filled each palm even before she got pregnant, straining against his chest. "Do you think that in India mothers crush their babies? It is only a neurotic WASP like you who believes it is healthier to let a baby cry himself to sleep in a cage like an animal."

Leslie is dying to bury his face between her breasts, but Surinder will not let him. Even after her mother has gone back to India, she is still complaining that she can't make love. When Leslie tries to transfer the baby to his crib, she insists that he leave her son — that is what she calls him, not our son or even Rajah, the name for which Leslie has relinquished Leslie Powers IV. "Leave my son on the bed. With his mother, who loves him more than life itself."

"More than me?" Leslie asks, half in jest, half wishing she would say it isn't true, that she still loves him the most, and take him in her arms before lust drives him to the cute nurse who is always smiling at him.

"Well, of course," Surinder says. "You are only the father. It is the mother who must teach the son love, religion, respect, how to care for the family."

"Religion?"

"What religion do you have to give him?"

Leslie has to admit that agnosticism isn't much of a religion, though the stories of the baby Jesus, Noah's ark, and the Ten Commandments might be worth passing down. *Thou shalt not kill*, he remembers, *thou shalt not commit adultery*.

When the days turn too cold to go outside without bundling Rajah up, Surinder begins to talk about taking him to India. "With my mother gone I have no help," she complains.

Leslie promises, "In another few years we'll be able to afford a nanny."

"In another few years my son will not need a nurse."

"Who says we have to stop with one?"

"It is true. In India they say that one son is as good as no son at all."

"That makes about as much sense as India has ever made to me, but I'll buy it," he says pulling her toward him.

"Get off me! You have no idea how that child exhausts me! I want to go home."

"This is home."

"Is my son to be raised in a world where no one wears the turban? At least let him visit India, where he can see the world he came from."

"He was born here," says Leslie. "He's American."

"American with a dark face. In India he will be the fairest child in the family. Everyone will come to see him. I must give my sister a present on the birth of my son, my aunts and cousins."

Leslie refuses to buy Surinder a ticket. Instead he drives the pretty nurse to a motel and keeps her up for three hours after her shift, enjoying the sweetest love he's ever known.

Surinder Kaur was created to make this story more original. But she escaped authorial control to marry a stock character. A return to Surinder Singh and Leslie Powers-Singh is necessary to avoid a plot even more familiar than seduction by a tall dark stranger.

"At least you're too old for a shotgun wedding," Leslie's sister said, overjoyed that Leslie was finally going to have a baby.

When prenatal tests revealed the fetus was a boy, Surinder called his mother in New Delhi and announced with all the confidence that technology can bring: "I will have a son at last." His mother asked him to send her a ticket: she would bring the child gold, a turban, gripe water for his colic, and the oil she had used to keep Surinder's skin from drying in the Delhi heat.

Even while the child was in the womb, squirming and tickling her insides, Leslie experienced a love she had never felt for a man, not even Surinder. After he was born, she found she could not return to work and leave the baby with Surinder's mother, though Bibiji stayed until the baby was crawling. Rajah, as they'd called him, was never out of someone's arms, even when he was asleep. Bibiji tried rubbing oil on his tender skin. She tried feeding him banana. Leslie couldn't make it clear that she could raise her child by herself.

Surinder took his mother's side.

"How can you agree with her?" Leslie asked. "She hasn't read Piaget, not even Spock!"

"Does a woman have to read European men in order to know how to raise a child? She had three children of her own."

Even before his mother went back to India, Surinder began to feel that this third marriage was over. Leslie was so involved with Rajah that she had no time for him. When she spoke of Rajah it was never "our son" or even "Rajah" but "my son. Leave my son alone! Let me feed my own son! Let me give my son a bath!" She curled up beside the crib on the floor of Rajah's room. Sleeping with Rajah had not struck Surinder as unusual. His daughter had slept in the bed beside his second wife. When he'd wanted to make love, he had simply carried the child into her own bedroom. But he couldn't carry Leslie.

He tried to tell himself that when Rajah was old enough to go to school, he would free himself from his mother's influence. He imagined Rajah in the best school in New Delhi, where *he* had gone — only boys, all in their green blazers and striped ties. American children went to school in sweatpants and jeans, even the girls. On the roads in front of schools, signs announced a "drug-free school zone." Why did the government have to assure the public that a school was free of drugs? On the news he'd seen police confiscating guns. But worse, he knew Americans who could not write a simple memo. More and more engineers came from India or China. Education had been half the reason that Surinder had sent his daughter back to India, and a first-class education was far more important for a boy than for a girl.

He didn't love Leslie, that was clear. She had been attractive once, a slim, well-preserved white woman, like Lady Mountbatten. He had thought a working wife could help him to support his family in India. But Leslie would not hear of going back to work. There was even less chance of her having another child. She was practically forty. The more Surinder looked at her, the more repulsed he was by her translucent skin, a face that reddened into splotches at the slightest emotion, her flat chest. His first and second wives had at least been young. The second had been buxom, pure Punjabi. When she gained, she carried weight below her breasts, a soft spot where Surinder had felt cushioned.

But he did not contact a lawyer. He'd seen enough American divorces to know what would happen: child lives with mother five days of the week; father supports them with a check so large that he can barely live himself; child goes to a school of the mother's choice; if she wants to raise him as a Christian, so be it, if she wants to cut his hair. When Rajah is eighteen he can live with the parent of his choice, he can grow his hair and wear the turban if he wants to, but by then he might already be in the habit of combing his hair back, running his fingers through it, shaving. Surinder put a plan into effect.

Leslie could have sworn there'd been half a gallon of milk in the refrigerator. "Where's the milk?" she asked.

"What milk?"

"Raj is going to get up from his nap. He'll want milk."

"I'll stay with him. By the time you bring the milk, he'll be up."

"He'll be crying for me. Why don't you — oh, you'll take too long," and she was in her coat and out the door by the time Surinder had his shoes on.

"Okay, Rajah Singh," he said, hoisting the sleeping toddler from his crib. No time to stuff him into his snow suit. He would not need it anyway. Surinder grabbed the box of diapers and carried Rajah to the car.

Leslie came home to an empty house. Rajah was not in his crib. She bit her hand and cried. She called the doctor. No, Mr. Singh hadn't called. She called the hospital. No toddlers in emergency at the moment, and no one had called an ambulance. She ran around the house shouting, "Rajah! Rajah baby!" Not a sound. She inspected the house for clues. None of Rajah's clothing was missing. She called the police. They put out a bulletin for a blue Mercedes, Surinder's license plate, but they reassured her: no one had reported any accidents, and if the child was with his father, there was nothing to worry about.

On her fourth trip into Rajah's room she noticed that the box of diapers was gone.

She rifled through Surinder's drawers. None of his clothing had been taken. But

Rajah's birth certificate, kept in her drawer with their hospital bracelets and her passport, was not there. She grabbed her passport and called Air India. They would not release the names of any passengers. She sat on the kitchen floor below the phone and cried.

She wiped her eyes and telephoned New Delhi. It was morning there. Surinder's sister answered.

"When are you expecting him?" Leslie asked.

"Who? Is everything all right? Is someone sick? In the hospital?"

"I don't know where they are. Hasn't Surinder called?"

"No. What is wrong? Is he all right? Is the baby? Are you afraid to tell us something?"

"Surinder took Rajah from his crib. Their papers are missing. Are you sure they're not on their way?"

"No," she said uncertainly. Leslie could hear her mother-in-law shouting by the phone.

She threw Rajah's clothes into two suitcases — warm clothes so that he would not be cold on the way back. On top of one bag she threw a change of underwear, a sweatshirt, a pair of jeans, socks for herself. Then she called her sister.

"Les," her sister said, "you love that boy more than you ever loved any man. Now get your ass to India and get him back."

She spent the night crossing the Atlantic, all day crossing Europe. The sun went down as the plane flew into Asia. She hadn't slept, she realized, since Saturday night, and she was scheduled to land early Wednesday morning. The plane was loaded with children, full-blooded, with the brown eyes and swarthy complexion of her own sweet Rajah. Everywhere she looked she saw him.

She got through customs at three o'clock in the morning. The airport was crowded — travelers, the people who had come to meet them, officials, police, luggage carriers — each small body blurring into the other. Leslie pushed through a forest of thin, brown men who kept grabbing for her luggage, their necks wrapped in woolen scarves. The black, smoky air was cold. She was glad to have her coat and Rajah's snowsuit. She shouted the address in English. One of the taxi drivers threw her bags into the trunk of a car so battered that she doubted it would ever reach the house. The taxi drove past crowds of people — at four o'clock in the morning — cows, goats, camels. Leslie felt sure she was hallucinating, gone to hell in this darkness teeming with ragged souls, when the taxi driver pulled up to a box-shaped, stucco, two-story house surrounded by others of its same shape and size. She thrust a handful of dollars into the driver's hand, carried her bags up to the door, and rang the bell. Her legs shook. A man began to sing in the distance. Trucks roared on the nearby highway.

Leslie heard her mother-in-law shouting. The door opened. She thought she saw Surinder in the darkness of a narrow corridor. With the last of her strength, she followed him through an open door. Her shins came up against the foot of a bed, and she fell forward and inhaled the breadlike smell of her peacefully sleeping son.

The potential for racism in a story of a dark man's kidnapping of his own mixed-race child necessitates escape to a safer narrative.

Leslie Powers III comes home to an empty apartment, no note, no explanation. When he doesn't find Surinder and his son in his bed, he checks Rajah's bedroom, his heart pounding in a relay between fear and the reddest rage he's ever known. Not a clean diaper in the entire apartment. He calls India.

"Where the hell's my wife?"

"She is not expected until two, three o'clock in the night," her mother says. "Is something wrong? Did she catch the plane? Did it leave on time?"

"How should I know?"

"You work so hard. You could not even take your own wife and child to the airport?"

"I didn't know my wife and child were going to the airport!"

"You need a vacation. You should have come with them."

"How can I come with them when they didn't tell me — Surinder didn't tell me she was leaving!"

"You can come at any time," she said. "No hurry. Only come before April."

"April?"

"It will be too hot for you."

He hangs up furious and stays that way all night. He takes a pill to sleep, gets up late, and rushes to the hospital, where even his lover cannot cheer him up. What right does she have to smile? His marriage is over, he's known that. But how is he going to get even holidays with his son?

He calls when it's morning in New Delhi. Surinder answers. "We are fine. You must not worry."

"Are you crazy? Taking off like that without even so much as a note? He's my son too, goddamn it! I want custody."

"Come to India," she says. "It's cold in Indiana. It's cold in Delhi too, but only at night. The days are warm in the sun. The sun is just coming up."

"Where's Rajah? Where's my son?"

"He's with Mummy, looking at the pigeons in the courtyard."

"I'll have you extradited for kidnapping."

"Do take care of yourself. Mummy says you should not work so hard."

"Are you listening to me?"

"Come as soon as you can. We miss you already. Good-bye!"

In India Surinder has to keep up the appearance of a loving wife so as not to give her parents the opportunity to reproach her for marrying for love. They believe that Americans have no respect for family; Leslie's own parents are divorced. Surinder thinks the fears that they expressed when Leslie came to India three years ago might have been justified, but she's too proud to say so. Besides, she's been insulted, not hurt. There's a difference. But she does not have to think about her husband's betrayal in India, where she can wear her saris, basking in the family's admiration for her fair-skinned, chestnut-haired son. She will have to apply a dot of eye liner behind his ear to counteract the evil eyes of jealous, dark-skinned cousins.

She arranges six yards of raspberry and lime-colored block-printed silk around her curves and lies on a cot in the courtyard. Rajah toddles on the scrubbed marble tiles after the Nepali houseboy she has known all of her life. Vegetable hawkers raise their tantalizing cries. "I must have Indian carrots!" she says, remembering the rich, red flesh that she has never been able to extract from pale American carrots. She smiles in anticipation of a sweet made from the red gratings, the rich, creamy milk, the rosewater, the sugar. She has to find a way to tell her mother that she isn't going back.

Anger follows Leslie through another day and half the night. He insults nurses, snaps at orderlies, barks at patients. When he finally gets off duty, he takes Cindy home and screws her on the very bed where his wife slept with the baby, all the while his mind racing: what diseases might Rajah get in India? He hasn't had a typhoid shot, his full course of hepatitis. Malaria cannot be prevented!

He asks a friend, who has already become an attorney while Leslie is still struggling with his internship, to send Surinder papers that will get him custody of Rajah whether she comes back herself or not.

But safe can be predictable. Conventions, expectations, even habits limit behavior, and in this story characters have behaved with little more originality than in life. Only Leslie Powers-Singh has been able to act with some ingenuity.

That first night in India, Leslie wrapped herself in her winter coat and lay alone on a short, narrow divan in the unheated parlor. She hardly slept, fearing that her son might be gone by morning. But after the pigeons cooing on the veranda, his voice was the second sound she heard.

Leslie's mother-in-law supervised the cleaning of a storeroom, where Leslie's suitcases were put beside a narrow cot covered with a thick, cotton quilt. The six-by-eight-foot room opened onto the courtyard, where Rajah played with Leslie's sister-in-law, Bibiji, the houseboy, and a babysitter who was always there. Surinder came and went without even looking in the doorway through which Leslie peered, curled up on the cot, the quilt wrapped around her. Rajah thrived on the attention of his grandmother and aunt. Paenji brought home toys and sweets, though Leslie forbade Rajah to eat the syrupy, deep-fried confections that he loved so much. Whenever Leslie tried to touch him, her mother-in-law shrieked. "In America you beat him," Paenji said, pulling Rajah to her chest. "That is why my brother had to save him." Leslie found it more and more difficult to get up from her cot. Her mind raced, feverish, while Rajah played. How was she going to get him back? He was never left alone. She could not even follow him outside onto the veranda in front of the house without someone running after them. If she grabbed Rajah and ran for a cab, someone would snatch him and call the police. What would she do then?

Leslie lay sick on her cot in the windowless closet. Bibiji stood in the doorway, glared at her, and had Paenji move her to a double bed in one of the warmer inside rooms. A doctor came to examine her and prescribed little white pills, which Leslie hid in her pockets. If she couldn't have Rajah, she didn't care if she lived or died.

In her illness she never heard Surinder, and she wondered if he'd left India. Paenji hovered by her bed, her dark eyes glistening with worry. Bibiji brought Rajah in to play. He was flourishing, his legs and arms fat, his skin glistening like burnished gold, as if he'd taken on the beauty of the women who came and went by Leslie's bed. Even her mother-in-law, at least seventy, looked resplendent in her silk harem pants and tunics, her brown hair streaked red with henna, her eyes as liquid as the gold she wore around her neck, her wrists, her fingers.

Leslie got up from the bed a size thinner than she'd ever been. In her jeans and sweatshirt she felt more like a man than a woman in this house where veils shuddered in the breeze and silks glistened in the sun. Paenji measured Leslie's shoulders, waist, chest, and height. "How slim you have become," she said. "If only I could give you some of my big tummy!"

Leslie wished she had ever been half as beautiful as Paenji and felt vaguely shy as this plump, buxom woman appraised her bony, white body.

One day she was napping with Rajah when Paenji came home with an armload of packages. "We have a holiday known as *Baisakhi*," Paenji said, and she held up a bright yellow tunic like the ones that she always wore. "All of us must wear new clothes."

"But this is silk," Leslie objected.

Paenji set aside the trousers that matched the tunic and held up a floor-length dress in a style reminiscent of Leslie's mother's generation. "As you are the sister-in-law of this house," Paenji went on, while her mother-in-law peered into the room, "I have had the tailor make you one of our suits. But as you are an American lady, Bibiji thought you might prefer a dress."

"I — I can't pay you," Leslie said. "I have some gold that I could sell —"

"Have I not just said you are a lady of the family?"

"The bangle that your mother gave me," Leslie said.

"You must wear it," Paenji said. "As a married lady."

Later, when Bibiji was no longer listening, Paenji shook her head at the delicate gold band on Leslie's wrist and whispered, "We would have given more, but my brother was already married."

"Where is he?" Leslie asked.

"Do not trouble yourself. Bibiji and I will pray for your health at the *gurdwara* — our temple. Finally the fog has gone. It is spring. But soon it will be summer. You must take care."

From the moment Leslie put on her bangle and the yellow suit, her position in the household changed. The babysitter put Rajah into Leslie's bed, and no one tried to take him until he woke up in the mornings. Bibiji shouted for the servant to bring Leslie's tea every morning and put her new clothes in a steel wardrobe next to the bed. Paenji continued bringing clothes, along with another gold bangle, thicker than the first. Leslie feared that Paenji could not afford the silks and jewelry on her salary as a sales clerk in a boutique and tried to tell her that she couldn't stay to wear them, anyway. Now that she was so far from home, she missed the job that she had left to raise Rajah, her time alone with him, even her car. She had been independent before Rajah was born, maybe a little lonely, but never to the point of pain.

Yet there were times she wondered whether single motherhood could compare with the support of a family like this. She had worked for years, would have to work eight, ten hours a day to support him when she got him back. Not for the first time she wished that her mother were alive, that her sister had not settled so far away. She wrote her sister, explaining that she didn't feel entirely at home in India, but that for the moment she had access to the only person in her life she had ever wanted.

"Stay," her sister wrote.

It is the author's responsibility to end a story. In this case, both stories.

Surinder Kaur sits in the sun just across New Delhi from Leslie Powers-Singh, reading the divorce papers her husband has sent. "Just let him try to take the grandson of a proud Sikh like my father," she mutters.

Rajah is climbing on Surinder's mother in the courtyard. "Is everything all right?" her mother calls.

"No," Surinder says. "My husband has been bewitched by a woman at the hospital. A white woman who cleans up the shit of others!"

"That this should happen to my own daughter!" her mother says, and both of them cry. "These white women are not to be trusted." Rajah whimpers as his grandmother wipes her tears with her *chuni*. "Even Lady Mountbatten bewitched our Pandit Nehru. Men are weak. You must go back. You must force him away from that girl, back into the family."

"What use can the family have for a man who would spend his nights with a woman who is not his wife?"

"It is as I feared: love between families so different is nothing but a trap. In India we fall in love after the marriage."

"When you have no choice," says Surinder, torn between agreeing with her mother and longing for her days of love, companionship, and pleasure. Surinder would like

197

to forget her childhood attractions to the country of Rajah's birth, the jeans and T-shirts her grandmother had brought her, the rock and roll she'd listened to. Her first steps into JFK had felt like walking onto the set of an American movie — the heroine escaping into a romantic adventure. But the longer that adventure had dragged on, the more she had longed for the brighter colors, the constant companionship of India. Microwaves, air conditioners, and cars are no substitute, ultimately, for tandoors, like the one in which her father roasts goat, chicken, and kebabs, or open courtyards that can be lived in even in January. And besides, her father had bought a microwave in Singapore. Her mother's room is air conditioned, and a generator outside the window keeps it going even when the electricity fails. India is coming up: an Indian company has even started making its own model of economy car.

So even though Surinder has grown up thinking that love is a powerful magnet that can draw a man and woman together against their duties to their families, Rajah has reminded her that love is blood. To abandon the country of her birth would separate Rajah from the best part of his blood forever. He is the little baby Krishna, incarnation of a god, stealing butter from milkmaids who love him. Surinder consoles her parents by reminding them that Rajah's birth has made him an American citizen, eligible even to run for the presidency of the United States.

As for Leslie, finally he has no choice but to let his lawyer draw up no-fault papers that allow Surinder custody if he can be absolved of paying child support. Otherwise, Cindy argues, how will they ever be able to support a family of their own? What if Rajah comes for college? Would they be expected to pay? Should they deny their own children in favor of a child halfway across the world?

Leslie grieves. He can hardly remember what his son looks like and cannot imagine him as the eighteen-year-old who might come back for college — the age his mother had been when Leslie had fallen in love with her. But Leslie has to agree with Cindy. This time he will do it right: finish his residency, save enough to buy a house, then have the kids. He will have a lot to do — baseball, soccer, football, basketball, swimming, and saving for at least one college tuition. By the time Leslie sees his son again, Rajah Singh Powers might be a resident at an American hospital, like the young Indian doctors that Leslie works with every day.

* * *

Switching genders, even crossing cultures, in this story has not succeeded in breaking the characters' habits, altering their traditions, or undermining society's expectations. The authorial experiment has failed. Without Surinder Singh, however, the story of Leslie Powers might be worth pursuing.

Hours spent lying in a darkened room as the ceiling fan dispelled the heat, Rajah snoring next to her, propelled Leslie through an Indian summer. She found privacy at night, sitting up with Rajah on the roof under a haze of stars. In the mornings Leslie and Paenji sat in the last bearable rays of the sun, Leslie brushing Rajah's hair and pinning it back, as Paenji had taught her. She was amazed at how fast Rajah had given up diapers. "How did you do it?" she asked. "His pediatrician said don't even try until he's three."

Paenji shrugged. "All children here are like this." She smoothed the light cotton print on Leslie's knee, transmitting a warmth surpassing the Indian sun. "Just the right length," she said. "That tailor is finally used to a lady of such height."

"I think the whole neighborhood is getting used to me," Leslie said. "They don't stare anymore."

Paenji laughed. "They call this the American house."

"Are you ever going to tell me where Surinder is?"

"We did not want to hurt you."

Was he sick? Had he killed himself? Nothing indicated that anything had gone wrong.

"He's gone," Paenji said. "We were afraid to tell you."

"Where?"

"There only."

"America? How can he leave Rajah when he went through so much trouble to bring him here?" Leslie asked, her hands rising involuntarily to her chest.

Paenji took Leslie's hands in her own. "When we saw how much you loved the child, we knew my brother lied when he said you beat him." Leslie's mother-in-law, listening from the doorway of the kitchen, added something in Punjabi. Leslie thought she recognized the words *nay* for no; *pyar*, meaning love; and *batcha*, child.

"He has always taken care of the family," Paenji said. "But he does not always tell the truth. He does not think before he acts."

"I should never have married him," said Leslie, realizing while her mother-in-law continued speaking that she'd never held another woman's hands, even her own sister's.

"Please don't go back," Paenji translated. "You are my own, dear sister. See how you look in a Punjabi suit!"

Rajah shouted, "My Mommy!" and wedged himself between the women. She could take him back; she was sure that the family would let them go if she decided to return. But if she took Rajah back, she'd have to deal with Surinder, put Rajah through some bitter memories. She drew a wriggling Rajah to her chest.

"Don't be afraid," Paenji said. "We will never let my brother touch the child — or you. In this family we are all women now."

How drawn Leslie felt to Paenji, more than she had ever been attracted to Surinder, perhaps to any man. "I must obtain a legal divorce," she said.

"We will manage," Paenji said. "Even if he stops sending money, we will manage."

"I can work," said Leslie. "I'm an engineer."

"India is in need of engineers," said Paenji. "So many of our students go abroad."

Rajah climbed on Leslie's lap as she leaned into her sister-in-law's embrace. Her mother-in-law hovered over them, chattering away, *pyar* and *batcha*, *batcha* and *pyar*. This community of women, Paenji, Bibiji, Surinder Kaur, was the warmest Leslie had ever known. She could not bring herself to leave until she'd played her part.

➳ The White Widow ➳

Sally would have sold the house the day after the funeral if her in-laws had only returned to India. Hermeet and Goodie had flown in from California for the cremation; that same evening they left. Sally's mother, father, and brother had also gone home when Sally told them she'd rather return to her practice than keep the wounds open by talking about Deshi, the plane crash, or what she would do next. Despite her father-in-law's crying and trying to pray in the family room, her mother-in-law's rising to embrace her whenever she walked through the door, she felt inconsolably alone. It had been six years since she'd miscarried the baby she'd conceived on her last trip to India. And her husband of twenty years had finally confirmed her fear of flying: his flight to Texas had developed mechanical problems, and the plane had crashed with no survivors.

Deshi's sisters dribbled in from England, South Africa, the Middle East, and India. For weeks they cleaned, cooked, and chattered about Deshi's excessive traveling, his lack of an heir, the thousand little things about growing up in India they suddenly remembered.

Twice she drove her sisters-in-law and their parents to the *gurdwara*. She sat listening to the lilting tenor of the priest accompanied by the mellow harmonium and tabla, more beautiful than their Western cousins, the accordion and drum. She almost overcame the awkwardness she always felt sitting on the floor, her feet bare, trying to keep her head covered with the end of the sari that her sister-in-law, Sita, had brought from India. She remembered marrying in red and gold, in just such a *gurdwara* in New Delhi. She found herself not wanting the music to end, not wanting to stand and arrange the sheer, white folds of her sari, more like a negligée than widow's weeds. She was reluctant to go back to the house, where every night she waited for the sound of Deshi opening the door.

When her sisters-in-law began returning home, Deshi's parents reacted to each daughter's departure with fresh tears, stomach aches, chest pains, and shortness of breath, for which Sally gave them antidepressants, antacids, and sedatives. She realized she should have asked them earlier to take their parents with them. She let the first sister-in-law go without broaching the topic. But on the ride home, the car full of the remaining sisters, she interrupted their Punjabi to ask who would see to their parents now.

The eldest sister, Pinky, a long-time resident of South Africa, was leaving in two days. She could not take her parents, she said, because their plans had not been made.

"Couldn't you have arranged to leave at the same time?" Sally asked, realizing too late that her question would divert the conversation.

On her next trip to the airport, Sally mentioned the subject again.

"Our mother and father will not abandon you," Sita responded. "We do not cast widows out of the house."

"I'm going to sell the house," Sally said. Now that her in-laws had removed the white sheets of mourning from the Persian carpet and the leather couch and love seat, she could contact a realtor.

"It's a good idea," said Jitty, Deshi's cousin, who had moved to California with her daughter. "Mummy and Daddy don't need so many rooms."

"And the house will remind them," said Sarah, who had Anglicized her name in Bradford, England.

"A complete change of place might console them," Sally said, as she inched with the traffic closer and closer to Long Island, where she and Deshi had once spent a vacation investigating potato farms for investment.

"You cannot be thinking of leaving this place," Sita argued. "They have become so familiar."

"I *am* leaving," Sally said. "After I sell the house."

"But Mummy and Daddy will not be able to adjust," said Pinky.

"That's why I want them to go back with one of you," Sally said.

"Not with me," said Sarah. "Health care in U.K. is a disaster. With you they will always have a doctor in the house."

"I have never been comfortable with your family's expectation that I keep your mother and father alive."

"Mummy and Daddy are old," Sita said. "How much time do they have?"

"In my experience," Sally answered, "you can never tell. They're in good health."

"They will keep you company," said Sarah, an expression of genuine satisfaction on her face.

"I don't want company," Sally said.

"You say that now," Sita said. "But it is very difficult."

"It's not the kind of company I need."

"Come to India," Sita said.

"You mean you'll take them?"

"How can I? Ram's family is traditional. They will not allow the girl's parents to stay in the boy's house."

At fifty, Sita was hardly a girl. "You'll have to get them an apartment," Sally said.

"They cannot live alone."

"I'll take them," Jitty offered. "It's just me and Nina. California weather will be comfortable for them. Sally, you come too."

Sally took a deep breath, so grateful to this woman who was not even her in-laws' biological daughter that fresh tears misted her eyes. But she could not cry while driving, would not cry in front of anyone, even family.

Sally could hear them whispering in the seat behind her. Jitty's voice tightened, rose, and finally broke.

"What's wrong?" Sally asked.

"It is nothing," Sita said, patting Sally on the arm.

The whispering continued well into the next morning, when Deshi's parents erupted into hiccoughing spells of sobbing. Sally had to sedate them before her sisters-in-law would tell her the truth.

"We advised Jitty not to ask them," Sita explained. "Jitty's daughter, Nina, is divorced."

"She only married Harry to get back into the country," Sally said. "Everybody knew it was a marriage of convenience."

"Even Jitty is not living with her husband," Sarah said.

"She is not our real sister," Sita went on.

"Your mother raised her. If the person who takes care of your parents has to be your blood, then I —"

"We will always love you as a sister," Sita assured her.

Jitty left the next day, apologizing profusely as Sally drove her alone to the airport. Sally heard the whole story: Jitty's inferior education compared to that of the other girls, her arranged marriage to a man who beat her, long visits with every cousin out of India, Nina's arranged marriage to a drug-abusing homosexual.

To spare Sally two more trips to Kennedy, Sarah and Sita rearranged their flights to leave at the same time. Their parents sobbed as they clutched these last children to their chests, Iqbal Singh's voice rising as he told Sita, "Give my love to Ram, Susheela and her husband, her little Papu, her mother-in-law and father-in-law, your mother-in-law . . ."

Poor Sita, returning to a house that had been full of responsibilities since the day she had married into it. The last thing she needed

209

was another burden. But her youngest sister, still in India, could help, and Deshi's parents still had more friends and family in India than in America. Sally spoke fast: "How much have your parents saved from selling their house in Delhi? Can they live on it? Deshi's life insurance will help."

"Why should Mummy, Daddy come?" Sita asked. "One day we will all be in America. Just let Chotu settle. Then I will make a house for my mother and father."

"Sita, by the time Chotu finally gets married, your mother and father could be dead. And how will you support yourself in this country? Where will you live? With Chotu? All of you?"

Sally felt strangely liberated. For fear of hurting Deshi, she had never spoken so directly to his sisters. She checked Sarah in with British Airways, then drove Sita around to Air India. She wished that she had simply bought two tickets for Deshi's parents, packed their bags, and driven them to the airport with their daughters.

Alone with Deshi's parents for the next few weeks, she looked for signs that they were making plans to leave, but their bags remained unpacked. They sat in the family room as usual, reading their prayer books. When she asked her father-in-law when he would like reservations for their flights to Delhi, he said, "What is the use? No one is left in India," and wept. Sally opened a fresh sample of antidepressants and took one herself.

Then the house sold, and Sally had so much to do — sell the furniture, write to communities in need of doctors, resign, inform her patients, clean out Deshi's closet — that she had no energy to make plans for her in-laws. Iqbal Singh asked her why so many men were calling on the telephone. Sally thought a moment. Then she laughed. It was the first time she had laughed since Deshi's death, and it surprised her.

Her mother-in-law gasped. Sally took a deep breath and explained that the callers might be coming to buy Deshi's car and suits.

Maybe it had been the laugh. Deshi had always insulated Sally from misunderstandings. Her mother-in-law broke into a stream of Punjabi that Iqbal Singh reduced to, "She does not want you to sell my son," tears rolling down his face.

Sally gave both of them another sample of Prozac, packed up the suits, loaded them into the Mercedes, and drove them to the old-clothes depository in the parking lot of the nearest supermarket.

As the giant garbage bag disappeared into the big, orange dome, Sally remembered how she'd lived before she'd married Deshi — alone, modestly, in a small, easily maintained space. She'd had plans to open up a practice in a remote, rural region, but Deshi couldn't make the million he'd always wanted in Appalachia or Mississippi. She sat in the supermarket parking lot enjoying the privacy of the car, recalling Deshi's permanently tanned, snake-hipped body, so small-framed that he did not meet the minimum recommended weight on the chart in her examination rooms. Had she unconsciously wished for the disappearance of that body, so as to dispose of the baggage that had come with it?

She told her father-in-law she was leaving.

"You are going to your own mother and father?"

"They retired in Tennessee," said Sally. "Mississippi is the next state south."

"You are going to Tennessee?"

"Mississippi. Americans don't live with their mothers and fathers."

"Mother and father can console," he said. "But a married girl should love her husband's mother and father as if they were her own."

"I know," she said. But without waiting any longer, she called the airlines and made her in-laws' reservations for the Sunday before the closing on the house.

On Friday, one of the neighbors called, a divorcé, and asked Sally if she was ready to go out.

Chuck was fair and pink-skinned, nothing like Deshi. She had waved to him every morning as he'd jogged by in his sweats. Sally wondered how she had gotten Chuck's attention, her disobedient hair going gray, her forty-five-year-old face clean of makeup — it was such an effort putting it on every morning.

When she told Iqbal Singh she was going out, her mother-in-law gaped at her above-the-knee skirt and heels. A rash of Punjabi followed Sally out the door. She felt sixteen again, dating against her own parents' will. Her mother-in-law's expression made her feel rebellious, though the thought of going home with Chuck burned the lining of her stomach.

Going out with Chuck, it turned out, told her in-laws what she could not say to them directly. When she came home, she saw their bags standing next to the door, packed, locked, and labeled. She took advantage of the moment and got Chuck to load them in her car.

"We must go to India," her father-in-law

said. "We are not these fantastics who throw the widow from the house." At this point Sally's mother-in-law began to dictate in Punjabi, which he dutifully translated: "You are young; you have not had children; if you had, my wife and I would take them so that you might marry." His voice broke.

"You don't have to say this," Sally said, and she thanked Chuck, who had already backed out the door.

Sally remembered every excuse she'd ever made for putting off pregnancy. She'd had far too much to do; Deshi was hardly ever home. Tests, after she'd lost the baby, had given her time to rethink the biological urge. While she had been thinking, cells had been dying without replacement, without fertilization.

"My wife and I do not think we could live with two Americans," her father-in-law was translating. "You work too hard. You have no Indian friends. In India, the whole house was full of friends. You do not speak our language."

"Sorry," Sally said. "That it didn't work, I mean. Your whole life . . . mine."

She would have burst into tears if she had not escaped to her bedroom. As usual, she couldn't tell them what she thought: that they'd given up too much by leaving India to live with their son. She spent the night feeling guilty that she had no sense of duty. She could not wait to get away. At the same time, she worried: what was she doing? Did she have the courage to change her job, her home, what life Deshi had left her?

Deshi's parents spent the morning gathering their hand luggage, cardigans, tickets, passports, and keys, praying on the threshold of the mother-in-law suite that they would never see again. Then Sally drove them into a much-too-early northeaster, over and past Long Island Sound, where both water and sky seemed bleached of the summer. She wondered why she hadn't thought before of going to India with the Singhs, where she could treat people far poorer than anyone in Mississippi. But India would make it impossible to forget Deshi, and only by forgetting him could she strike out in a different direction, toward a life she might have lived if she had never met him.

At the gate, Sally's mother-in-law pulled her to her chest, sobbing as if she might never see Sally again. Iqbal Singh urged her to come to India, and Sally promised. As she walked into the drizzle again, the mist creating such a glare that she had to squint to see past the stream of arriving buses and taxis, she heard the sudden roar of a jet. Automatically she turned, too late to see anything in the blinding sky. A horn

blared and she leapt onto the concrete island between the lanes. She had never had time to drive
Deshi to the airport. She suddenly remembered
him coming back from a trip not a full twenty-
four hours after the limo had picked him up.
He'd barged through the door shouting, "The
meeting was canceled!" Sally left dinner burning on the stove to throw her arms around him
before her in-laws could embrace him first.

A dull pain gnawed at the flesh between
her ribs. She sat down on the concrete, her head
folded into her lap, and cried, grateful that she
still lived near New York, where no one rushing
by to catch a plane would stop to ask if she was
all right, what had happened, what she might
have lost.

She cried long enough to feel a hand at
her elbow. A man's voice, inflected with an ac-
cent she couldn't recognize, asked, "Do you need
a doctor?"

"I am a doctor," she said. Without even
looking at him, she got up and made her way
across the parking lot.